THE JIGSAW PUZZLE

THE JIGSAW PUZZLE

BY

E. J. WARDE

VICTORY PRESS
EASTBOURNE

Filmset in Great Britain for Kingsway Publications Limited, Lottbridge Drove, Eastbourne, E. Sussex BN23 6NT by Richard Clay (The Chaucer Press) Ltd., Bungay, Suffolk and printed by Fletcher & Son Ltd., Norwich

CHAPTER ONE

THE PUZZLE ARRIVES

It was Tony and Peter's Great-Aunt Emily who brought the puzzle. The boys were not a bit pleased when, on the last morning of the summer holidays, the postman brought a letter from her to say that she would like to call that afternoon to see them and would catch the four-thirty bus home again.

"Oh, Mum!" Peter looked at her in dismay. "That means we'll have to put on clean shirts and brush our hair and scrub our nails and answer politely when she asks silly questions about school. The Chesters got back from Norway yesterday evening and we wanted to hear about their holiday."

"Well surely you can see Dick and Vincent tomorrow? You know your father likes you to be kind to his old aunt. She has been very good to you all your lives, and we are almost the only relatives she has left in the world."

"Ye-es. And she usually tips us a pound each when she comes. That'd be a bit more towards my motorbike." Tony, who was fifteen, was saving as hard as he could, because his parents had promised that if he could find a quarter of the money they would put the other three quarters and he could have a moped next year. "But all the same, we can't see the Chesters after this afternoon because they are going off to their gran in Aylesbury tomorrow and straight back to boarding school from there. Couldn't we scoot round there after lunch, Mum, and get back in time for tea? Aunt Em will be able to tell you about all her latest aches and pains before we come."

Mrs Rathbone considered and the boys waited hopefully. "All right. As long as you are back by a quarter to four, and if you are dirty and untidy you clean up properly before you come into the sitting-room. But Aunt Em does like to see you, so you won't be late, will you?"

Of course they promised, and two o'clock found them with their friends in the big, rambling house at the other end of the village. Tony and Dick settled down to look at maps of the route the Chesters had taken, while the two twelve-year-olds discussed less serious aspects of the trip.

"I only wish the slides had come," said Dick. "We sent two lots back to be developed about ten days ago, and they ought to be some of the best. I did hope they'd have come before we went back to school. It'll be rotten to have to wait until half term to see them."

But a little later Mrs Chester came in from doing some shopping. "Here are the photos, boys. I called in at the post office and they had just come through."

"Oh, grand! Dad won't mind if we put the screen up and run through them with Tony and Peter, will he, Mum?"

"No, I'm sure he won't, if you are careful with them. I'll wait and see them this evening when he gets in."

Tony glanced at his watch and saw that it was ten past three. "We mustn't stay long, but I'd love to see some of them. Your dad is a very keen photographer, isn't he?"

"Rather! And he's jolly good, too. You'll see."

The slides were fascinating. Beginning when they were on the boat approaching Norway, they showed members of the family in all their activities and always with a wonderful background. Peter and Tony were enthralled.

"There! That's the last one of this lot. I suppose you'd better cut along home now, hadn't you, if you have to be in before four-thirty?"

"Four thirty! We've got to be back by quarter to four." Tony glanced again at his watch and found to his horror that it still showed three-ten, as it had done when Mrs Chester brought in the slides. He looked at the clock on the wall. "Four-twenty! Pete, we'll have to rush. We'll only have time to say hello and good-bye."

But although they ran all the way the bus pulled out as they reached their home. They waited rather apprehensively for their mother to come in. At first she was very angry indeed, but at last she did believe that it had really been accidental.

Their father took a more serious view. He had hoped to get back from his work in Selchester before his aunt left, but this had been impossible, and he was afraid the old lady would feel neglected. He gave them a lecture on selfishness and lack of consideration.

"You will both write to her and apologise for your bad manners," he finished. "In fact, you had better go and do it now, before supper."

Peter, no letter writer at the best of times, looked very dismal, but Tony nodded. "Righto! We'll go up and do it in our room, Pete. If we sound repentant enough she might write and send us her usual tip."

The last part of this speech was not intended for his parents' ears, but Mum's hearing was sharp. "Really, Tony, do you think of nothing except money! Oh, before you go I must show you this. Aunt Em bought this jigsaw at the white elephant stall at her local village fête. She intended to give it to the people at the old folk's home near her house, but she wants to know first if all the pieces are still there. She thought you two might enjoy making it up, and then she will collect it when she comes at Christmas. You had better say in your letters that you will enjoy doing it."

"But, Mum, it must be huge!" Peter looked at the size of the box in horror. "I should think there are at least a thousand pieces."

"I think she said there are two thousand. You'll be able to get on with it on some wet evenings."

"Mum, how can we?" Tony decided to try a little calm reasoning. "You know there's nowhere in our room that we can leave it lying about. If it's as big as that it wouldn't even go on our table. And anyway, I shan't have time for any silly jigsaws. I've got prep to do."

If he thought that this provided a watertight excuse he was mistaken. Mr Rathbone looked up from his evening paper.

"Tony, Peter, come here!" He waited until they were standing before him. "Now listen to me. That jigsaw is to be made before Aunt Em comes at Christmas. You can use the trestle table which I have for wall papering, and put it in the old dark-room under the stairs. I shall not be doing any decorating or developing any photographs for the next few months. If you are careful you will be able to lift the table top out here while you are working. Now go and get your letters written, or your mother will be ready with supper before you have finished."

Tony, whose favourite subject was English, quite enjoyed letter writing. He explained about his watch having stopped, said how sorry he was to have missed his aunt, filled two pages with a description of some of the transparencies they had seen at the Chesters' house and signed it with a flourish.

"There, that ought to be good for a tip. I should think. How are you getting on, Pete?"

"Awful!" Peter flung down his pen in disgust. "I can't think of anything to say. I've put about your watch stopping and that we meant to be home in good time. Oh, have you said about the jigsaw?" He groaned. "Think of it! Two thousand pieces!"

"I forgot about that. You'd better put that we shall enjoy doing it and that Dad says we can use his wall-papering table top." Tony looked over his brother's shoulder. "Pete, your spelling is ghastly. Meant is m-e-a-n-t, not m-e-n-t, and wrist starts w-r, not r-w!"

"Bother! I knew there was a 'w' in it somewhere. English is a silly language anyway." He crossed out the offending words, making the sheet even more untidy than before, then looked at it doubtfully. "Do you think I'd better write it again?"

Tony grinned. "You might just as well. If Dad asks to see it he'll certainly tell you to do it again after supper. Here, I'll put the bit about the jigsaw on the bottom for you and then you can copy it."

Peter stuck his tongue out of the corner of his mouth and concentrated and at last the task was done. After supper the boys were afraid their father might suggest making a start on the giant puzzle, but fortunately there was one of his favourite programmes on the television and they were able to escape. Tony went up to the bedroom, where he spent an enjoyable hour reading a book on motorbike scrambling, and Peter hurried to the shed behind the garage, where he was busy trying to construct a model of an air liner. Peter Rathbone might seem a complete duffer when he handled a pen, but those same awkward fingers were extraordinarily deft with even the smallest pieces of a plastic model.

CHAPTER TWO

SPREADING OUT THE PIECES

Tony could have been excused for saying that he would not have much spare time for making jigsaws when term started. The village of High Steadington was twelve miles from Selchester, where both boys went to school. They were the last pupils to be dropped by the school bus, and by the time they had had their meal it was after six o'clock, and then he usually had the best part of an hour's prep to do.

But on that first day of the term – the beginning of the new school year – the routine was not properly established and he had no work to bring home. Peter, three years younger, never had much prep and usually none at all.

It was just as well! Mum had cleaned up the long trestle table and it was leaning against the wall, beside the old cardboard box, waiting until the supper was cleared. She spread a thick cloth on the polished dining-table and told the two boys to lift the long white-wood one on to it, then she herself broke the sticky tape which sealed the box and turned out the pieces in a heap.

Unexpectedly they were of plywood instead of the usual thin cardboard, and at the sight of this even Tony brightened up.

"Oh, that will make it easier to do. Those wretched flimsy ones fall apart at the slightest jerk." He picked up a dozen pieces and started to put them face upward. "But, my word, they are all grey! I suppose it's sky –

that looks like part of a cloud – but if it's all like this it will take months."

Peter, equally dismayed, dug into the pile and let a handful trickle through his fingers. There were one or two patches of scarlet and he found one with what looked like part of a wheel, but certainly the majority seemed to be either grey or green.

"Oh well, I suppose we'd better make a start," he said. "Let's spread all the bits on one end of the table, Tony, and when we come across something which looks like edge we can keep it separate. Once we get the outside done we shall know how big it is. There's a Henry Hudson programme on the telly at eight. If we get it all spread out, Mum, that would be enough for this evening, wouldn't it?"

"Yes, that would be a good start. Pass me the box, Peter, and I'll brush it out, so that it will be ready to use when the puzzle is made up."

The old hatbox was lined with newspaper, which she crumpled up and threw in the wastepaper basket, but later on, when the table top had been carried carefully into the cupboard under the stairs which Dad used as a dark-room, and the boys and their parents were settling down to watch the detective programme, Dad noticed it and fished it out.

"My goodness, that's an old one. The *Selchester Advertiser* packed up years ago." He glanced at the date at the top of the sheet. "April, nineteen forty-two! Somebody must have had that puzzle stowed away somewhere for the best part of forty years."

He threw it away again, but Tony, who had thoughts of journalism as a career, picked it out and took it upstairs when he and Peter went to bed.

"Seems funny, doesn't it," he said, as he opened the flimsy sheet. "When that was printed Dad was five and Mum was two! That was when there were air raids on

Selchester. Oh, that's rummy; there's a bit here about Sedgebury." He ran his eye down the little paragraph and whistled. "Phew!"

"What's up? Someone we know in Sedgebury?" This was a little village four miles from High Steadington and, because of the river which ran beside it, was a favourite picnicking spot with the brothers and their friends.

"No, but you remember when we were there last month we saw the remains of that old cottage right in the woods?"

"Yes, you said it looked as if there had been an explosion."

"Well, I was right. Listen to this. 'Attack on Sedgebury.' 'The village of Sedgebury had a mir-aculous escape during the raid. One of the German bombers, which for some reason had not dropped its load on the city, discharged its lethal cargo close to Sedgebury before making good its escape. But the sum total of damage done was the excavation of three large craters in the long meadow owned by Farmer Joliffe and the destruction of a small cottage which stands in the woods beyond the village. The cottage is owned by a Mr Cunliffe; said locally to be a recluse, who came to Sedgebury five years ago, but fortunately he is away from home at present, undergoing an operation for ap-pendicitis in a Bournemouth hospital. Like most West Country villages Sedgebury is crammed with evacuees, and had the bombs fallen a quarter of a mile farther to the east it is almost certain that there would have been considerable loss of life. See page five for our reporter's account of his interview with Mr Cunliffe, whom he visited in Bournemouth yesterday.'"

"Is page five there?"

"No, this is the outside sheet; one and two, and seven and eight. Poor chap, it must be pretty awful to have your home blown to bits while you are away."

"What is a recluse?"

"Somebody who lives by himself and wants to be left alone. It sounds as if he didn't have many friends in the village, or they'd have been more upset about the cottage being destroyed."

Peter grunted, not much interested, but Tony found his thoughts returning quite often to the remains of the old cottage, and he wondered what Mr Cunliffe had done when he got out of hospital. It was a pity that he couldn't get hold of a copy of the paper, but as it wasn't even printed any longer there didn't seem to be a chance.

At the end of the English lesson the next day he remembered that the master had lived in Selchester all his life, and sometimes wrote articles for the West Country papers.

"Excuse me, sir!" He caught up with the elderly teacher. "Can you spare a minute?"

"Of course, Tony. What can I do for you?"

Tony looked at him affectionately. Mr Smith was a strict disciplinarian and woe betide you if he caught you slacking, but he was never too busy to answer a question. He explained about the sheet of newspaper. "What I wondered, sir, is whether back copies of papers are stored away somewhere – file copies, I mean, just for reference purposes – or whether when a paper is no longer being produced they are all destroyed. Did you ever see the *Advertiser*?"

"Yes, we used to take it. It was a weekly which started up not long before the Second World War and was bought out by the *Gazette*. In fact, I went there a few months ago when I was researching for an article. I hope you will find what you want. Perhaps you will write an essay on the subject for me?"

Tony thanked him, grimaced behind the master's

back at the thought of the essay and hurried off to his next class.

The next thing was to go to the offices of the *Gazette*. Where were they anyway? If they were close to the school he might be able to fit it in during his lunch break, but Selchester was a big place and if he had to go to the other side of the city it would take too long.

He found the answer to his problems when he looked at the telephone directory at home that evening.

Selchester Gazette, Offices, Number Ten, Drake Street; telephone Selchester 44851.

"Dad, where's Drake Street?" he asked.

"Drake Street? Just round the corner from my office. Why do you want to know?"

Tony bit his lip. Would Dad say he was wasting his time? Then he had a brainwave. "I've got to write an essay for Mr Smith, the English master, and it means hunting through some old editions of the paper, so I was wondering whether I'd have time to get there and back after school dinner, but it would take the best part of twenty minutes each way."

"More than that, I should think. But I've got a client coming to see me at five o'clock tomorrow, so I shan't be leaving for home until at least half past. If you like to go to the *Gazette* place when you finish school, and then come round to the office and wait for me, I'll bring you home."

"Oh, thanks, Dad. I'll do that. That'll be fine."

"There you are, young man. Nineteen forty-two, you say? They would be somewhere in that corner. Take great care how you handle them, if you please, and replace everything exactly as you found it."

The elderly man who had conducted him to the cellar beneath the *Gazette* offices shuffled away up the wooden steps and Tony turned to his task. Finding the copy he needed was quite simple; they were tied in bundles covering six months each and he needed the first week in April. He turned to page five, but at first he could not see any article with a heading about Mr Cunliffe or the cottage at Sedgebury.

Then he found it. 'Well Known Explorer Loses His Home.' 'Our reporter, going to visit the old gentleman whose home, as reported on Page one, was demolished during the air attack on Selchester, received the surprise of his life when he found himself at the bedside of Mr Samuel Cunliffe, the well-known explorer, whose discoveries in South America hit the headlines some years ago. Mr Cunliffe, probably the best known living authority on the ancient civilization of the Incas, was far from pleased when he was recognized. He explained that he had come to Sedgebury in search of peace and seclusion in which to write about his work, and he was only persuaded to allow his identity to be revealed when he learned that he had no longer a home to which to return. The manuscript of his book, he said, was now in the hands of a typing firm in London, and there was nothing else of value at the cottage which could be destroyed by enemy action. He added that he was not such a fool as to leave anything he had wrested from the Peruvian hills in a place where curious villagers or light-fingered marauders could obtain access to it. This, our reporter assumes, was a reference to several visits paid to the cottage by Mrs Oke, the postmistress of Sedgebury, and to the occasion, reported in the Advertiser three weeks ago, when two of the evacuees, returning to the village in tears after a visit to the woods, complained that the old gentleman had seen them near the cottage and had chased them off, brandishing a heavy walking stick. An Englishman's home is his castle, we are told, but it is understandable that the villagers of Sedgebury will not be altogether sorry that this particular castle will not be occupied again.'

"Surly old beast!" Tony took a notebook from his pocket and started to write down the main points of the article. Then, his pencil poised over the paper, he stopped. If Samuel Cunliffe was so well-known it was odd that they hadn't studied his book last term when they had had a lesson on the Incas. He must look up the notes he had taken at the time. He paused again when he came to the bit about the Peruvian hills. It sounded almost like buried treasure! But of course, if there was anything hidden away beyond the reach of the bomb, then the old chap would have come back and collected it before departing to some other hide-out in another part of England.

He folded the newspaper very carefully and went to put it back in its place, but then stopped as the heading of the next issue caught his eye.

'Death of Well Known Explorer!'

'Mr Samuel Cunliffe, whose cottage home, as reported in last week's issue, was destroyed in the air attack on Selchester, has died in the hospital in Bournemouth where he had undergone an operation for appendicitis. It is understood that the cause was heart failure. He was seventy-eight. Obituary on Page six.'

Tony turned quickly to page six, but there didn't seem to be anything very interesting in the obituary notice. Born in Canterbury, then the schools he had attended, Edinburgh University and all his various degrees, married in eighteen-ninety-four, Evelyn Macdonald, one son, Bruce, born in nineteen hundred. Evelyn died nineteen hundred, so that was presumably when the son was born. Perhaps that's why old Samuel seemed to have been a crotchety old chap. He served in the First World War but spent most of his remaining years in South America. But there were no details about what he had done in Peru, so except for dotting down the dates and that sort of thing, Tony felt that it didn't help much. He tied the tape carefully round the bundle of papers, went back upstairs, thanked the old clerk and hurried off to his father's office.

Later on, in his bedroom, he looked at his notes. The most important question which needed an answer was this. If Mr Cunliffe had died without coming out of hospital and therefore had not been able to go back to Sedgebury, what had happened to his South American treasure?

CHAPTER THREE

MAKING A START

Saturday was sunny and warm; as good as any week-end during the summer holidays. Mr Rathbone had to go into the office for an hour or two, so his wife decided to go in with him and do some shopping.

"What are you boys planning to do?" she asked, as they cleared the breakfast table.

"I'm going out on my bike," said Tony promptly. "We can't waste such a gorgeous day. Could we take some sandwiches, Mum, and get home by teatime?"

Their mother raised no objection, and by nine o'clock they were on their way. "Where are we going?" asked Peter, and when Tony said Sedgebury he added excitedly: "Oh good! Did you find out anything interesting?"

"Rather!" As they pedalled at a leisurely pace along the quiet country lanes Tony told him what he had learned from his visit to the newspaper offices. "Then yesterday in school I spent the free time after dinner hunting through the pages about the Incas in the Encyclopaedia Britannica. They mention Samuel Cunliffe's explorations, and quote a bit from one paper he read to some society or other, but there's nothing about a book. So what happened to it? Surely, if he was such a top notch chap on the subject his book would be one of the textbooks on the Incas?"

Peter wasn't much interested in the book. "Do you really think he had a lot of Inca gold buried somewhere near the cottage? What are you going to do, Tony? It's an absolute jungle of brambles. It would be hopeless to try to dig, even if you knew where to begin."

"I know. I thought we might have a prowl round the village and see if we could find somebody who remembers the chap."

"But it was donkey's years ago."

"Not all that long really. Grandpa fought in the Second World War and so did Great Uncle Edward."

"Well, rather you than me. You'll get your head bitten off!"

As it turned out, they received some unexpected help in their investigations. A boy came out of one of the cottages and Peter braked sharply.

"Hello! Tony, this is Stephen Underhill. He is in my form at school. Do you live here, Stephen? You are new, aren't you?"

"Yes, we came a month ago – just Mum and me – because Dad had to go abroad. We were in one of the flats which belong to his firm, and they want Dad to be their representative in Australia, so of course we had to move out to make room for the man who took over his job in Leicester."

"Couldn't he take you and your mum with him?"

"Not yet. For the first six months he will have to travel a lot and go to all the different parts of the country. Then he hopes to be based in Perth, and we shall probably join him."

"What made you come to Sedgebury? It's a long way from Leicester."

"Well, when Mum was a girl her parents lived near London and she was evacuated down here. She didn't stay long; the worst of the bombing was over by the time she was seven; but Mrs West, who took her in, was jolly kind to her and they always kept in touch. She's old now and she has gone to live with her daughter in Selchester, but she lets this cottage, so Mum has rented it for as long as we need it."

Peter looked at Tony and waited to see what he would say. "That's interesting, Stephen. Peter and I were reading in an old newspaper the other day about the time some bombs were dropped right here in Sedgebury. Was your mum here then?"

"I don't know – she never told me so – but you can come and ask her if you like. She's in the kitchen."

Mrs Underhill was baking, but she welcomed the boys with a smile and seemed glad that her son had found a friend. Tony guessed that the boy was finding life a bit lonely in Devon.

"Mum, Tony Rathbone said that there were bombs in Sedgebury during the war. Was that when you were here?"

"Yes, although I'd forgotten all about it. I remember going out to look at the huge holes in the farmer's field. But how did you hear about it, Tony? It was such a long time ago."

She was most interested in the story of Tony's investigations, but she was a little doubtful when he mentioned his idea of enquiring in the village. "I don't know whether anybody will be able to tell you much," she said. "The most likely person would be old Mrs Oke, who used to run the village shop and post office."

"Oh yes, there was something about her in the article. Mr Cunliffe told the reporter that he had hidden his treasures where no curious villagers would find them."

Mrs Underhill laughed. "Yes, she is a nice person, but she does like to know all about everybody. I can imagine that an old gentleman living like a hermit would have aroused her curiosity. But she is very kind all the same, and would do anything to help anybody in trouble."

"You can't talk to her this morning," said Stephen.

"There's a bus into Selchester on Saturday mornings and I saw her getting on to it."

"Oh well, let's go and have another look at the cottage," said Peter, feeling rather relieved. "Would you like to come along, Stephen?"

"Rather! You don't want me, do you, Mum?"

"No, dear, you run along. Would you two like to leave your bicycles round by the shed at the back? What time do you have to be home?"

The boys explained that they had brought a picnic. They left their sandwiches in their saddlebags and set off.

When they had seen the cottage one afternoon in August they had given it only a casual glance, but now they looked at it with much more interest. Not that there was much to see. It was very small and had probably consisted of one room downstairs and one up. The walls were very thick, but all that remained was one which was stronger than the rest because it had a chimney running up it and the remains of the other three. Brambles, as Peter had said, were growing all round, but they could see some large slabs of stone which had paved a path leading to the door. Encouraged by this, Peter cut a stout branch from a nearby tree and trimmed it into a useful weapon with which he beat the trailing undergrowth away.

The floor inside was also stone and so was the large fireplace. There was no furniture, but an old iron hook hung down the chimney and a heavy black kettle stood in the hearth.

Tony looked round with a frown. "It's rummy!" he said.

"What is?" asked Peter.

"Well, he was away and the cottage was almost blown to bits, so I suppose the furniture would have been smashed, too. And yet there's none left; not even a bit of a table or a chair. You could understand it if the house had caught fire, but it didn't because there are still those bits of beam sticking out from that wall and they'd have been burnt. But what an extraordinary place for an educated man to bury himself for years. No electricity, no gas, not even water unless he fetched it from the river."

"Would that be fit to drink?" asked Stephen doubtfully.

"Well, I wouldn't like to, but I suppose if he'd been an explorer he would have been used to worse than that. I wonder if he had a garden. What I mean is, if he buried his treasure, then a corner of his garden would be the most likely place. Oh well, we can't do anything here, although I must say I'd be glad to get my hands on a pile of Inca gold!"

Stephen looked at him doubtfully. "But even if you found some, it wouldn't belong to you, would it?"

"I don't see why not. He's been dead for ages. Anyway, if we did find something of value I'd take jolly good care that nobody else got their claws into it. Come on, let's go and paddle in the river."

There was a pool upstream of the cottage, on the far side of the woods, where at one time there was said to have been a ford. There had been a lot of rain since August, making it much deeper than it had been then, and they had good fun.

"What a super place," said Stephen. "I wish we had something to make a raft with. We could float right through the woods and come out in the meadow near the village."

Tony shook his head. "I wouldn't like to try it. I've never seen the river running so fast and we'd be out of our depth most of the way." He saw that Stephen was unconvinced and, feeling responsible for the younger boys, went on quickly: "Come on, let's dry off in the sun. It's much colder than I expected."

Peter rubbed his feet with a tuft of grass and put on his sandals. "Shall we go back along by the river?" he suggested. "It would be interesting to find out if there is a path from the cottage to the river, then we'd know if old Mr Cunliffe fetched his water from there."

But when they came to the place where they could see the old chimney sticking up among the trees there was no sign of any break in the undergrowth. They were about to continue their journey when Peter stopped.

"There's water running somewhere," he said.

Tony hooted. "No! Surely not!"

Peter laughed, too. "Ass! I didn't mean the river. I can hear water splashing." He knelt down and peered over the bank. "Yes, it's spurting out about six inches down. There's a bit of piping. Perhaps there's a spring somewhere and the old chap used to get his water here before it reached the river. That would have been cleaner, wouldn't it?"

Since none of the boys knew anything about springs there didn't seem to be anything more they could do, so they went on their way and were soon back at the cottage.

They had finished their picnic and were wondering how to spend the afternoon when Stephen glanced out of the window.

"There's old Mrs Oke now, getting out of Tom Joliffe's car. He must have brought her back from Selchester. Perhaps you'll be able to ask her about Mr Cunliffe and the cottage after all."

Peter looked doubtful. How could you go up to an old woman and start asking questions? But Tony was determined to have a try. He watched Mrs Oke go into the little village store.

"Is there anything you need from the shop, Mrs

Underhill? I haven't brought any money, or I'd go and get some stamps."

She smiled and went to her handbag. "I need two airmail letter cards, Tony, if you'd like to get them for me."

"Thanks. That will be fine. Coming, Pete? Don't if you don't want to; it might be easier for one person."

"Okay, you go. What are you going to do, Stephen?"

"Mum and I are going blackberrying. Mr Joliffe said we could go round the hedges in his pastures. Like to come and give us a hand for a bit?"

So while they armed themselves with baskets Tony made his way slowly along the road to the shop. Now that the time had come he began to be doubtful. How could he start? And what could he do if someone else was serving in the shop?

Well, Mrs Underhill wanted the letter cards. He pushed open the door with its jangling bell and went in. A man was behind the metal grille which showed the post office part.

"What can I do for you, young man?"

"Two airmail letter cards, please."

The man opened a drawer and started to look through the contents. "Now where on earth has she put them? Trouble is, sir, that the wife usually looks after the shop, only she'm in the city today. Could you come back on Monday?"

"No, I don't live here. I just came on my bike for the day."

The man behind the counter pulled open another drawer. "I guess she must be out of them. Ma! Could you come a minute?"

The door behind the counter opened and the old woman came through. Her son explained.

"Now, Jack, you know we can't sell post office stuff

on a Saturday afternoon. 'Tis agin the law. We'm closed for all they things. Sorry, young man, but there it be."

"That's all right, Mrs Oke. I'm sorry I bothered you. I expect Mrs Underhill will come and buy them on Monday."

He turned to leave, but the man stopped him. "If you'm a stranger how come you know Ma's name?" he asked.

It was the chance he wanted. "I was reading about Mrs Oke in the paper a few days ago, and it said she was the postmistress here. As a matter of fact I wanted to ask her a few questions – if you don't mind, Mrs Oke."

"Me! In the paper? I ain't seed nothin' 'bout me in the paper."

"Er – no, it wasn't a new paper – it was a very old one – about the time when the bombs fell on Sedgebury."

Mrs Oke was quite ready to talk; in fact once she started it was difficult to get a word in about the things he wanted to know.

"I wanted to ask you about the cottage in the woods," he said at last. "We found it when we were picnicking in the summer, and today we went and looked at it again. The paper said that you called to see Mr Cunliffe sometimes." Tony was not without tact and he added quickly: "I expect you wanted to help him, didn't you, as he was living there alone?"

"Ar, that were it, young sir, but if you'd a seen 'im and 'eard 'im, you'd a thought I just come quizzing like, that rude 'e was. But there, the poor ol' gennel-man's dead, so the less said the better."

"My brother and I wondered why there was nothing left in the cottage; no broken bits of furniture or any-thing?"

"Well now, that were a mighty queer thing. Farmer Joliffe – not Tom Joliffe what's there now, but 'is feyther what ran the farm in they days – 'e said as 'e reckoned as that there bomb just caught the roof of the cottage and fell on the garding. It blowed the walls to smithereens, like you see now, but the bits they fell outside like. Then, arter the old gennelman died, some lawyer fellers come down – from Lunnon I reckon they be – an' they fixed up for all 'is furniture and such like to be carted away. O' course lots of it were smashed a bit, but 'twas good stuff, an' in they days – what with the war and the bombings and such-like – I reckon folks was glad to get hold of anything, and they'd 'ave mended it up."

Tony wanted to find out if anybody had discovered the hidden treasure, but he didn't know how to put it. "You didn't hear, I suppose, whether the lawyers took away anything very valuable? In the paper, where I read about it, there was something about Mr Cunliffe having hidden away the secrets he'd brought back from South America."

"Secrets!" The old woman chuckled. "Ay, all the folk in Sedgebury read that bit, an' a mighty 'unt they 'ad. Took spades an' shovels an' shifted all they gurt 'unks of stone, looking for treasure. An' much good it done 'em. All they found was 'taties an' carrots! An' a good thing, too! The Good Lord don't intend for us to go takin' what don't rightly belong to us, nor to get rich by finding a lot o' money. We'm put on this earth to work for our livin', that's my belief, an' what good would it 'ave done if someone 'ad found gold or jools or such-like at 'Well Cottage'? They'd just 'ave bin fightin' an' argyfying 'bout it, an' ended by killin' each other, I don't wonder."

With which the old woman stumped back into her cheerful sitting-room behind the shop and Tony thanked her son and returned to the Underhills' cottage.

Later that evening, when, at Dad's command, they reluctantly brought out the puzzle and worked at joining up all the edge pieces Tony looked at Peter and chuckled.

"Going round the edge! That's what we've been doing today."

"What on earth do you mean?"

"Well, don't you see? It's just like this wretched puzzle. We've found the bits that go round the edge, but we haven't any idea yet what we shall find in the middle. It might be quite exciting, and so might our hunt for Samuel Cunliffe's hidden treasure."

CHAPTER FOUR

LOOKING FOR GOLD

Although they had finished the edge of the puzzle
and now knew that it was nearly four feet wide by three
feet deep, there still seemed to be just as many pieces
left outside the square. Tony and Peter, faced with the
task of putting in an hour on the job after supper on
Sunday, looked at it with distaste and perplexity.

"Of all the dull pictures!" said Peter in disgust. "The
top is grey, except there where the trees stick up; there
is green right down the left side, and a different shade
of green along most of the bottom."

His father chuckled. "Well, that leaves the right
hand side, old chap," he said. "What happens there?"

"Grey half way down, then a bit which might be a
road, and then more green. No wonder it was on a
white elephant stall. I shouldn't think anybody has
ever finished it."

"Then you and Tony will be the first, won't you?"
said Dad calmly, and returned to his book.

Mum, who was knitting, looked up. "If I were you,
boys, I'd pick out some pieces which are not grey or
green and try to put them together. Even if you can't
see at first just where they fit in the picture they would
give you some idea of what it is about." She stuck her
needles into the wool and came to look over their
shoulders. "There are quite a lot of white pieces, and
that one has part of a window on it, so there must be a
house. I can see some bright red bits, too."

"Bags I the red," said Tony. "Perhaps it's a car or
something."

They worked for a while in silence, but then Tony straightened his back and stood up. "I've got it! It's a coach. I want another bit of the passengers on the roof. How's the house coming on, Pete?"

"I'm not doing the house. I'm looking for the bits of gold. There seems to be quite a lot of it, but I haven't the foggiest idea what it's going to make. It's just gold bars."

Tony laughed. "Bars of gold, eh? I hope you find them!" But neither he nor Peter was thinking about the puzzle.

During lunch break the next day Peter went to the library to try to get a book on model making, which had been out during the previous week.

"I'm sorry, it isn't back yet," said the elderly librarian. "But there is a new one in which might interest you. 'Model Aircraft' it is called. It's by a man called Curle."

"Thank you." Peter went over to the shelf where the books written by authors whose names began with 'C' were kept. Chamberlain, Cobbold, Cratch, Cunliffe, Curle – ah, that was it. He was just picking it up when the significance of the one next to it occurred to him. Cunliffe! Perhaps this was the one Tony had been talking about. But when he took it out he found that it was by somebody called Barbara Cunliffe and was about needlework! He put it back in disgust and went to the desk.

"I hope it will be helpful," said the librarian.

"Thank you. Oh, I wonder if you can help me about something else? Have you ever heard of a man called Cunliffe? Samuel Cunliffe, his name was, and he was an explorer in Peru."

"The Inca chap, you mean? Yes, of course I've heard of him. He was one of the greatest authorities on the Inca civilization who ever lived."

"I suppose he wrote a book on it, didn't he?"

"Unfortunately, no! Or rather, it is believed that he did write one, and that he got as far as sending the manuscript to London to be typed, but this was during the war and the building where the job was being done was destroyed, so the manuscript was lost. This would not have been so terribly important; Mr Cunliffe could have written it again; but unfortunately he died shortly afterwards."

"What a shame. So nobody knows what he really discovered?"

"We know about his earlier journeyings. His companion and assistant, a man called Palmer, wrote a book about that. In fact, we have it in the library. 'Old Peru', it is called. You will find it in the section on South America, if you want to look at it. But old Samuel was a queer fellow – very difficult to get on with – and he and Palmer quarrelled. Palmer returned to England, but Cunliffe stayed in Peru on his own for another five or six years. Then he, too, came home, with the intention, I believe, of writing his book, but as I said this was lost through enemy action during the war."

"What a beastly shame. So now nobody will know what wonderful things he found?"

The librarian beamed at him. It was not often that one of the boys from school was interested in such a worth-while topic. Mostly they seemed to want detective or space-age fiction.

"I'm afraid not. But Mr Palmer's book gives quite an interesting picture of the ancient Inca civilization, and as he was a much younger man it would probably be somewhat easier to understand than Samuel Cunliffe's would have been."

Well, perhaps Tony would like to read it, thought

Peter. So he went to the shelf and returned with the little grey-covered book, the librarian stamped it and the model-making one and he hurried back to school.

He gave it to Tony on the way home in the bus and after a while he heard an excited exclamation. "Look at this, Pete!"

Peter turned from his study of wing spans of aircraft to see a picture. The text underneath read: 'One of a pair of gold beakers found by Mr Cunliffe and the author in the remains of the old Inca temple. Presented by Mr Palmer to the British Museum.'

"Um! But what's the good of that? It's in a museum."

"Yes, but don't you see, you ass? It stands to reason that if Mr Palmer had one, then old Samuel had the other."

"So you think that's what he'd got hidden away somewhere? It doesn't look much."

Tony breathed an exasperated sigh, thankful that they were now almost alone in the bus. "If you could bring your microscopic brain to bear on the subject for a moment, you might realize that this is gold and centuries old. It must be worth a fortune."

The bus stopped and the last trio except for the Rathbones got off.

"It seems to me that I've got a lot more sense than you," retorted Peter indignantly. "What do you think would happen if you did by chance find the vase or whatever it is and tried to sell it?"

"That's a point. But if he had one of these he probably brought home a lot of smaller things – coins perhaps, or gold nuggets. Well, here we are. Don't mention this to Mum or Dad. They know I'm mugging up the Incas for an essay, that's all."

Peter, more interested in balsa wood models which could be made to fly than ugly gold vases which they

weren't likely to find, nodded and they hurried home
to tea.

As soon as the meal was over he hurried out to the
shed, taking the model-making book with him, and
started to check up on what he had which he could use
and what he would need to buy. He decided to start
first on one of the simplest aircraft, driven by a very
thick rubber band. He had once made a boat from
balsa wood, but this was some time ago and it hadn't
been a great success. Now he hunted it out from a box
of odd bits and pieces. Yes, the hull would make the
body of the aircraft, so all he'd need of the wood would
be enough for the wings. He spent a happy evening
shaping the body and wings, and the next day during
lunch he bought everything else that was necessary.
Fortunately he had had a birthday three weeks before,
so he wasn't hard up.

For the next two evenings he spent every available
moment in the shed, and by bedtime on Thursday it
was finished. Now came the great moment. Would it
fly? Unfortunately the back garden was nearly all cul-
tivated, with neat rows of vegetables and fruit bushes;
even the small patch of lawn had two apple trees on it,
which made it useless for the purpose; and the front was
all roses and things like that. In the end he decided
reluctantly that it was too dark anyway and he'd better
wait until tomorrow. He could take it to school and try
it on the playing field. But then if it didn't work the
other chaps would laugh. He had bragged about his
model and Harry Brown had bet him it would crash.
In the end he decided that he would wait until after tea
tomorrow and then take it up to the top of the hill,
sneak into one of Mr Trent's fields and try it there.

He knew his parents would not approve of this idea.
Dad had had a row with Mr Trent when some of his

sheep, grazing in the field behind the cottage, had scrambled through a gap in the hedge and eaten a lot of cabbages. The farmer had declared that it was Mr Rathbone's fault because the hedge wasn't thick enough and Dad had said that it was Mr Trent's responsibility to keep his animals from straying. Since then Dad had given orders that the boys were to stay off Mr Trent's property. But there wasn't any other suitable place, so he'd just chance it.

As it happened Mum made it easy. "Peter," she called after tea, "the post goes in five minutes. Will you run along to the box and post this for me. I do want it to go out today."

"Righto, Mum!" Peter took the letter, ran to the shed where his precious model was lying on the bench, tucked it under his coat and went off to the box outside the shop. Then he went on up the hill.

The pasture for which he was aiming was right at the top, where there was a stiff breeze blowing. Peter took a quick look round to make sure nobody was in sight, then climbed over the gate. Looking down across that field and the next he could see the farmhouse, and beside it the long greenhouse where Mrs Trent grew carnations and chrysanthemums for the market. Peter had once heard Mum say that Mrs Trent probably made almost as much from her flowers as the farmer did with his milk.

Getting well away from the hedge, so that there was no danger of smashing his model, Peter wound the propeller, twisting the rubber band with each revolution. Then, pointing it slightly upward, he let it go. It turned upside down and pitched towards the ground, and it was only by throwing himself forward that he managed to catch it before it crashed. He faced the other way and tried again, but this was no better. He consulted the book.

'The machine flies best in a light breeze,' it said. No wonder he couldn't get it going, up here in a howling gale. Perhaps it might go better if he went down to the lower field, but from there he would be in sight of the farmhouse windows.

Then he saw Mr Trent come out of the house, walk to the garage and drive his big yellow car round towards the front, where he was joined by his wife before moving on, through the gates and into the village. Peter waited until the car had come into sight again beyond the cottages and then set off for the lower field. The farmer and his wife lived alone, he knew, so nobody would see him trespassing.

Once in the sheltered lower level he began to master his model. It really was a beauty, behaving more like a glider than a propeller-driven craft, dipping and picking up again, gradually losing height until it landed gently on the grass. He was thrilled. He'd certainly take it to school on Monday and show Harry that he was wrong. He glanced at his watch. Just one more flight and he must go home.

Secure in the knowledge that the farmhouse was empty, he didn't realize how close he was to the tall hedge which separated the garden from the field. As he let his little craft go a gust of wind took it. It swept over the tops of the hawthorns and dipped sharply. There was a tinkle of breaking glass and then silence!

CHAPTER FIVE

GREY SKIES

What on earth was he to do? If he went home and said nothing Mr or Mrs Trent would be sure to find the remains of the model and they would guess that this had caused the smash. But would they know that it was his? With a sinking heart he remembered that Mrs Trent had been in the shop a few weeks before when he was discussing model-making with the shopkeeper. Yes, they'd know it was his all right. Besides, Mum and Dad knew he was working on one and they might ask how he was getting on.

Could he get it back? A gate led from the field into the garden and he looked over the top of it. Yes, there was a jagged hole in the roof of the big greenhouse. The aircraft must have gone right through. Well, there was nobody about. If he was to try to recover it he'd never have a better chance.

Half a minute later he was at the door. It wasn't locked, and it was the work of a moment to hurry along between the two rows of plants to the place where pieces of glass lay scattered on the ground. His model had caught among the leaves, and except for a piece broken from the tail fin, seemed undamaged. He recovered the plane and scurried out.

It was as he was closing the door that his eye fell on a heap of stones close at hand. Quick as a flash he picked one up, went in again and left it beside the broken glass. That would put them off the scent. He retraced his steps and returned home, as he had come, with the aircraft hidden under his coat. During a very wet week-end he made a new tail fin and on Monday he took it to school to prove to Harry Brown that his model could fly just as well as he had forecast that it would.

It was at tea that the blow fell. "Oh, Arthur, what do you think!" said Mum. "You know that Mr Trent and his man Bill Gorse haven't been getting on too well lately?"

"Yes, and I'm not suprised," said Dad. "Trent is a difficult fellow in many ways, but he's a good farmer, and Bill Gorse is a slacker. What is the latest news about them?"

"Well, last Friday Mr and Mrs Trent went out for an hour, and when they got home they happened to see that little monkey Charlie Gorse sneaking out of the garden."

"Been after apples, I expect."

"That's what Mrs Trent thought, but when she went to lock up the greenhouse she found that he had thrown a big stone through the roof!"

"Serve the Trents jolly well right," said Tony.

"No, Tony, I can't agree with you." Dad looked serious. "Two wrongs don't make a right. Wilful damage won't improve the position for Bill Gorse. It will only make Mr Trent more difficult to please than ever. Where did you hear about it, Doris?"

"Mrs Trent was in the shop when I went along this morning. I think the worst part of it is that the boy won't own up. He admits that he took some apples, but he denies throwing the stone."

"I should think Mr Trent would probably give him a licking if he did own up," said Tony, "but he can't prove that Charlie did it if nobody saw him, can he?"

"No, he can't," said Mrs Rathbone. "But that's not all. Mr Trent, so his wife says, has decided that he cannot put up with the Gorse family any longer. He

GREY SKIES
37

has given the man a month's notice, and he is going to invite one of his nephews to come and join him at the farm and perhaps go into partnership with him. I know Bill Gorse isn't a very good worker, but I can't help being sorry for his wife. There are two little girls younger than Charlie and a baby boy of six months old. It will be awful for them if Bill can't get another job quickly."

Peter was appalled. Of course the model aircraft going through the glass had been an accident, but he had been trespassing, and, worse still, he had tried to cover up by putting the stone in the greenhouse. But he couldn't very well let Mr Trent sack his man for something Charlie hadn't done.

He was still hesitating when his father spoke. "I should think Trent is glad of an excuse to get rid of the chap. He's as hard as flint, and the fact that the Gorse family may suffer hardship won't weigh with him. It's as well nobody saw the poor little beggar. Trent would probably report him to Constable Sykes, and Bill Gorse would have to pay for the repair."

At that Peter's mind was made up. The only thing he could do was to keep mum. If Mr Trent hadn't taken this chance to get rid of the Gorse family he'd soon have found another, and if he, Peter, owned up then Dad would have to pay for the repair.

Glad to have come to a decision, he tried to forget the whole incident, but during the next few days it was surprising how difficult this proved. When he and Tony were waiting for the bus the next morning he saw Mrs Gorse at her cottage gate watching Charlie going off to the village school. She waved to the child and turned to go into the house, and Peter saw her put her handkerchief to her eyes as if she was crying. On Wednesday, coming home in the bus, he overheard another boy, whose father was a farmer, talking about the number of

out of work farm labourers, and how impossible it was
for his dad to afford to employ another man, even
though there would have been plenty of work for him.
Worst of all, on Thursday he learned that little Julie
Gorse, who was four years old, had fallen and broken
her leg, and was in hospital in Selchester. Peter wished
with all his heart that he had confessed his crime at
once. Now, having left it nearly a week, it was impossible.

On Friday morning, going towards his classroom,
Peter found Stephen Underhill beside him. Since their
visit to Sedgebury he had become quite friendly with
Stephen, who, he discovered, was not only a keen
model-maker, but was also interested in the same sub-
jects as he was, such as maths and science.

"Hello, Peter! I say, have you got anything fixed for
this weekend?"

"Nothing special. Why?"

"Well, it's my birthday tomorrow and I'm getting a
super model; I chose it myself as my present from Dad.
Mum wondered, if you hadn't got anything better to
do, and if your mother didn't mind, whether you'd like
to come and spend the weekend with us."

The thought of getting away from High Steadington
and leaving his feeling of guilt behind was a tremen-
dous relief. "Oh yes, I'd love that. I'm sure Mum won't
mind. What time shall I come?"

"Mum said she'd drive over to pick you up – at
about ten o'clock – and take you in to school on Monday
morning. She teaches at the Smith Street Infants
School herself, so she takes me in with her. But if your
folk have got something else fixed perhaps you could
telephone to Mrs Oke at the post office and she would
send us a message. We aren't on the phone ourselves."

Peter's mother was quite agreeable. "It will be a nice
change for you, Peter. You have been looking a bit

tired this week. I know you moved up at the beginning of the term. Perhaps you are finding the work rather hard."

Tony scoffed. "Don't you believe it, Mum. He doesn't even get any prep yet. I'll bet he only wants to go to get out of doing a bit to that beastly jigsaw on Sunday evening."

"Well I don't then," retorted Peter snappishly. "I'll do my share this evening."

He did, too, but as he spent an hour filling in a few tiny patches of the grey skies – which, he felt, reflected the greyness of his own unhappy life – it couldn't be said that the picture looked much better at bedtime.

Saturday morning was great fun. In addition to the model of the Royal Yacht, Britannia, which Stephen had bought with his father's birthday money, his mother had given him a small metal vice which could be attached to any table; a thing Peter himself had wanted for a long time, as the one in their shed was a very clumsy wooden contraption. Peter, at Mum's suggestion, had given Stephen a small model kit of a Spitfire, which he happened to know the other boy wanted for his collection. They went out to the little shed behind the cottage and started work, and by dinner-time the hull of 'Britannia' was taking shape but they had finished the tube of adhesive.

"Never mind, we can get one at Oke's. Let's find out if we've got time to go before we eat."

But Mrs Underhill had the meal just ready, so they washed their hands and sat down at the kitchen table. Peter was a little surprised that they said grace before eating – not just 'for what we are about to receive' etc., which old Aunt Emily expected the Rathbone boys to murmur when she visited their home, but a simple prayer thanking God for their good food and for the

happiness of Stephen's birthday. He didn't say anything, of course, but it seemed odd. They were such
ordinary, jolly people, not goody-goody at all. Then he
forgot about grace and attacked the big plateful of
chicken with a good appetite. It was followed by a
lemon meringue pie which was Stephen's favourite,
and by the time they had finished they were both feeling full up and in need of some exercise.

"What are you going to do this afternoon, Mum?"
asked Stephen as they helped with the washing up.
"Peter and I want a walk."

"I'm going up to Hilltop Cottage to take old Miss
Danby some crab-apple jelly I made yesterday. If you
like to come that far with me you could go round by
the old mill and back along the river bank. You said
you wanted some more glue, didn't you?"

Peter, who had lived all his life in the country, had
never walked before with people who came from a big
town and were so much interested in all growing
things. Stephen and his mother stopped to watch a bird
in flight and to try to identify it, and stood quite still to
watch a bee getting pollen from a spray of late honey-
suckle.

They left Mrs Underhill and went on until they
reached the river some distance below Sedgebury, then
followed its winding course until they got back to the
village. Mr Oke, minding the shop as he usually did on
Saturday afternoons, welcomed them cheerily and was
most interested in their account of the model, but
Stephen had to tell him where to find the adhesive.

"Last time I bought some, Mrs Oke got it from that
shelf where the soap powders are kept," he said.

"So 'tis, to be sure." He put his head on one side and
looked at Stephen with a smile. "I call to mind the wife
saying that your ma come buying icing sugar and mar-
zipan a few days ago. I reckon 'tis your birthday about

now, eh?" Stephen nodded and held out a pound note which he had received as a present from one of his aunts. "Well, I hope you'm having a good time and your ship will make up all right. Though how you can fix all they fiddley little bits and pieces beats me for sure."

Stephen laughed. He took his change and waited while Mr Oke insisted on finding a paper bag for the glue, explaining that it was rather sticky, then the two boys hurried back to the cottage, their enormous dinner forgotten and quite ready for tea!

The meal over, Mrs Underhill spread newspaper on the kitchen table and the boys brought their modelling indoors, which, as the light was fading, made it much easier. The new vice was fixed in place, with a thin piece of wood under it so that it didn't mark the table top, and Stephen went to the bag for the glue. As he tipped it out a piece of paper fell on the floor and Peter picked it up. It was a pound note.

"Oh, goodness!" said Stephen. "Poor Mr Oke, he gets in such a muddle when he is in charge of the shop. I'd better take it along straight away. I know they balance the till on Saturdays. Shan't be long. Can you do a bit of the bridge?"

"Yes, of course I can, but –"

"But what?"

"Well, Mr Oke knew it was your birthday. Perhaps he tucked that in as a birthday present."

"No, I'm sure he wouldn't have done that. He's always very nice, but after all, he hasn't known us for very long."

"But all the same, I don't see how you can take it back. You say the shop will be shut, and you'd probably have to give it to his wife or his mother which would make him look an awful fool, wouldn't it? I'd hang on to it, if I were you. That book on model-

making that I got from the library; the one I showed
you at home this morning; costs about a pound and
you'd be able to get a copy of that."

Peter picked up the note and smoothed out the
creases. "It did look a super book," he said, "but I can
borrow it from the library when you take it back." He
picked up his jacket, which he had thrown over the
back of a chair, and walked out.

As he had promised he was back quite soon. "What
did he say?"

Stephen laughed. "You should have seen them. They
were all sitting round the table in their living-room,
trying to balance the money from the till. They were
very grateful. Old Mrs Oke said I ought to have half of
it as a reward, but I couldn't take it, of course."

"Why on earth not?" Peter was genuinely surprised.

"Well, you can't take a reward for being honest –
not if you are a Christian."

"How do you mean? Most people in England are
Christians. At least, I suppose there are more Moslems
and people like that than there used to be, now that
there are so many Asians living here, but surely there
are still more Christians than anything else, and I don't
believe one in ten of them would have missed the
chance of keeping a pound note when it was handed to
them like that."

Stephen laughed. "You remind me of the man who
lived next door to us in Leicester. There was a mission
being held not far from us and Dad asked if he was
going. 'What, all that stuff!' he said. 'Not me, I'm a
Christian; I don't need converting and I don't hold
with having meetings in halls and such-like. I go to
church. That's the proper place for religion.' But
actually the only time he ever went to church was to
the carol service just before Christmas."

Peter was silent, remembering that they, too, had

gone to the carol service at High Steadington because Mum knew some of the parents of the kids who were singing. He wondered just what Stephen meant by being a Christian. It seemed as if it was something which helped him to be honest enough to return a pound which he could quite easily have got away with keeping. Just as he himself had got away with smashing that rotten greenhouse. Oh bother! Why did he have to think of that?

Stephen broke the silence. "Well come on, let's get the funnels in place." After that they worked steadily, until Mrs Underhill came and said it was time to stop because she wanted the table.

CHAPTER SIX

TOO DIFFICULT WITHOUT HELP

There were two beds in Stephen's room and Peter was soon in his. He snuggled down and then remembered that Tony had given him a job to do. "Oh, Stephen!" He turned over and looked towards the other bed, only to see his friend kneeling beside it with his hands clasped and his eyes closed. He halted uncomfortably and turned away again.

Two or three minutes later he heard the creak as Stephen got in. "You were going to ask me something, Peter," he said.

"Yes. Tony wanted to know if you'd heard anything more about old Samuel Cunliffe and the ruined cottage."

"No, I'm afraid not. Does he still hope to find treasure?"

Peter told him about the book he'd borrowed from the library and Tony's guess that Mr Cunliffe would have had the second gold beaker. "But as old Mrs Oke said the people from here dug up the whole garden I shouldn't think he's got a chance of finding anything. I expect he'll soon forget it. Good night. It's been a super day."

He expected to go to sleep at once, but, perhaps because Stephen had pulled back the curtains and the room was full of moonlight, he couldn't get off. He could see by the stillness in the second bed that Stephen was sleeping soundly, but at the end of what felt like hours he was still wide awake.

He tried to pretend that he didn't know the reason, but an inner voice told him that this wasn't true. During the busy days he was able to forget the wretched episode of the broken greenhouse, but once he was quiet thoughts of the consequences of his deception came flooding back. He wished he was like Stephen. Faced with the chance of getting an extra pound he hadn't hesitated. He wouldn't even take a reward for being honest. Peter wished he knew exactly what the other boy had meant when he talked about it making a difference if you were a Christian, but he hadn't known how to ask.

He found out more the next morning. After breakfast Mrs Underhill looked at him with a smile. "Peter, Stephen and I have a little Bible reading each morning at this time. Would you like to share his Bible? I don't suppose you have brought one with you. It only takes a few minutes."

It was a story he had heard in school, about a man called Zaccheus, who wanted to see what Jesus looked like. He was very short and he couldn't see over the shoulders of the people in front of him, so he climbed up into a tree and looked from there. He didn't expect Jesus would see him, but He did, and He told Zaccheus to come down because He wanted to stay at his house that day.

That was as much as he remembered, but they read a little more; where Zaccheus told Jesus he would give half his money to poor people, and if he had cheated anybody he would repay four times over.

Peter thought that sounded a bit steep. "Do you think he had cheated anyone, Mrs Underhill?" he asked.

"Yes, I think he probably had. He collected the taxes for the Romans and it says he was very rich, so I think that he probably took more off the people than the Romans asked for and kept the rest for himself. But of course, when he was converted he wouldn't have wanted to do that any more."

"Converted? What's that?"

"Well, I suppose the easiest way to explain it is to say that he turned round. He had been living his life in his own way, looking after himself and his interests and not bothering about anybody else. Now he had met Jesus and with His help he was making a fresh start."

She didn't say any more about it and Peter didn't ask, but several times during that day he found himself thinking about the story of the little man who promised to pay back what he had got by cheating. It wasn't quite the same as he himself had done; he hadn't actually got anything – he'd only wriggled out of what would have been awful trouble – but he'd certainly cheated the Trents and poor Charlie Gorse and his family.

Although it was more than half way through September it was a lovely day, so they took tea and drove ten miles up on to Dartmoor. They found a spot sheltered from the wind by rocks and when they had eaten, Stephen, never still for long, decided to climb the nearest hill.

"Coming, Peter?"

"I haven't quite finished my drink. I'll catch you up."

He waited until Stephen was out of hearing and then looked across at Mrs Underhill. "Do you think he did it? Zaccheus, I mean."

"Did what, Peter? Climbed up in the tree?"

"No. Paid back what he owed. It would have been awfully difficult to go to somebody and say: 'Look here, I charged you six pounds for your taxes and it ought to have been five. I'll pay you back four times over.' And then give him four pounds."

"Very difficult indeed. In fact, I shouldn't think he

could have done it if he hadn't had the Lord Jesus to help him. But if you remember, Peter, in the last verse of that story Jesus reminded the people that He had come to seek and save. When somebody becomes a Christian; when he or she tells Jesus Christ that they know they aren't strong enough to do everything right; (and there isn't anybody in the world who can do that; Jesus Himself was the only person who lived a perfect life) then He will help them."

Seeing that Peter still looked puzzled she waited a moment and then explained a bit more. "Perhaps I can put it better by using myself as an example. When I was a girl I was very hot tempered. I used to quarrel with my brothers and sisters and with my schoolfriends and get into hot water. Sometimes – perhaps on New Year's Day – I would make up my mind that I really would keep my temper, and for a little while I would be quite good – until something upset me, and then I was as bad as ever. Then one day, when I'd been sent to bed in disgrace, I talked to the Lord Jesus. I told Him I was sorry and asked Him to help me. I was converted – I turned round – I became a Christian – you can call it which you choose."

"And then didn't you ever lose your temper again?"

"Yes, I did, sometimes, although never as badly, I think. But when I did I was sorry and ashamed, and Jesus helped me to apologize and try to put things right."

Peter sat looking at his cup of tea, now quite cold. Then he gulped it down and stood up. "Thank you for explaining. Er – can I help you to pack up?"

"No, thank you, dear. You go and catch up with Stephen. We shall have to start back in half an hour."

"Righto, I'll tell him." He started off up the steep slope. He was glad that he knew what Stephen had meant by being a Christian, but he knew that it would be much too difficult for him.

When he got home after school on Monday Mum wanted to know how he'd enjoyed his weekend and he was able to give a glowing account of the good time he'd had. Then Dad suggested that it was time he got on with the puzzle.

"I don't think you put in more than a dozen pieces on Friday," he said, "and that's not many out of two thousand."

"I'll help you bring it out before I start my prep," said Tony. "I did my whack yesterday." He seemed a bit excited about something, and Peter wondered what was in the wind.

When they brought the long trestle table out into the brightly lit sitting-room he gasped. The top five or six inches – grey sky and trees – was done and the chimneys of a long house were taking shape.

"Tony! You must have put in hours on it."

"Pooh! It just shows what can be done with a little concentration!" Then he grinned. "No, actually Mum and Dad suddenly got interested and they helped. Mum was wizard at it. I'd never have got anywhere by myself."

"Yes, we helped over the most difficult part. Now it's up to you to carry on," said Dad.

Tony went upstairs to do his prep and Peter set to work on the puzzle with renewed enthusiasm. But then something his mother said to his father brought him to an abrupt halt.

"Oh, Arthur, I saw Mrs Gorse today and asked her about little Julie. She is getting on quite well and is to be allowed home next week, although she will have to go in to Out Patients. But she told me something almost more important. Mr Trent has decided to give

Bill Gorse another chance. Provided Charlie will own up to throwing the stone through the roof he will forget the incident."

"That's good. The shock won't have done Bill Gorse any harm, and that little imp Charlie will be more careful in future."

Peter stood like a statue. This seemed worst of all. Now Charlie had got to own up to something he didn't do. In desperation he swung round to tell his parents the truth, but Dad had returned to watching the telly and Mum was looking at the paper and somehow the words wouldn't come. He wanted to get away somewhere by himself and think. But Tony was in the bedroom, and if he went into the kitchen Mum was sure to come out for something, and she would wonder what on earth he was doing. Then he noticed that one of the pieces of the jigsaw – a corner at the top – was missing.

"I think we must have dropped a bit of the edge on the darkroom floor," he muttered, and almost ran from the room. There was no electric light in the cupboard under the stairs which Dad used as a dark-room, but he picked up the torch which was kept in the hall, darted inside and shut the door. Then, sitting on one of the trestles, he tried to think what to do.

Mrs Underhill had said she didn't think Zaccheus could have returned the money unless Jesus Christ had helped him. She had also told him that Jesus had helped her to keep her temper. A gulp – half laugh, half sob – broke from him as he remembered Tony's remark about the puzzle. 'Mum and Dad helped. I'd never have got anywhere by myself.'

Would Jesus Christ help him if he asked Him? He was twelve and he'd never thought much about Jesus before, so it seemed pretty awful to ask Him now. But then Zaccheus had been grown-up and Jesus had helped him. And the story had said that he came to save people who were lost.

"Jesus!" He spoke aloud in an effort to say just what he wanted to. "Jesus, I'm sorry I was such a rotten beast. Please give me the courage to try to put things right, like You did Zaccheus. And help me to go on – sort of – sort of depending on You and talking to You, like Stephen does, so that I won't let You down." There was a long pause, and then he remembered that all the prayers they had said at school ended in the same way, so he added: "for Jesus Christ's sake, Amen."

He sat there in the dark for a minute or two, then lit the torch and hunted round until he found the small piece of the puzzle and went back to the sitting-room.

Mum looked up from her paper. "Did you find it, dear, or do you want somebody to help you?"

"Yes, I got it, thanks. But – but will you help me to know what to say to Mr Trent?"

In the astonished silence that followed Peter blurted out the whole miserable story. Dad was furious, of course – Peter had expected that – but Mum was shocked and upset, which was harder to bear. It ended by Dad getting out the car and driving him up to the farm, where another very unpleasant interview followed. One of the worst parts was that he realized that Dad was ashamed of him and also hated feeling small. It might not have been so bad if he and the farmer had been on good terms, but to have to admit that his son was to blame was very difficult indeed.

"I'll pay for the damage, of course," he said, going to his pocket and taking out his cheque book.

"No, Dad, I'd rather do that myself – please. I've still got the five pound note Great Uncle George sent me for my birthday. Will it cost more than that to mend it, Mr Trent?"

"No, Peter. The glass cost one pound twenty-five,

and I did the job myself."

Peter calculated. "Oh, that's good. So if I pay five pounds that will be restoring four-fold, like Zaccheus?"

The farmer was obviously familiar with the story. "That's it. All right, Peter, slate wiped clean." He held out his hand and Peter shook it awkwardly. Then, more surprisingly, he shook hands with Dad and walked with them to the front door.

"What on earth did you mean about Zack Somebody-or-other?" demanded Dad, as they drove back.

Peter told him, and explained a little diffidently how he had asked Jesus to help him too, like He had helped Zaccheus.

Dad only grunted. "Well, as old Trent has been decent enough to call the incident closed I'll say no more either. Now you'd better cut along to bed or you'll be fit for nothing in school tomorrow. Good night. Sleep well."

He did, too!

CHAPTER SEVEN

IT'S A WELL

It was an announcement on the radio about three weeks later which revived Tony's flagging interest in the old cottage at Sedgebury, where he had almost given up hope of finding buried treasure. The price of most motor vehicles, including motor-cycles and mopeds, was going up by ten per cent in November.

"I'll never manage to save my share of the money if they go on like that," he grumbled to Peter at bedtime that evening. "I wish I could think how to make some extra cash. When you think of the stuff which must be somewhere round that old Well Cottage it's just too maddening. I think if it's decent on Saturday I'll go and have another squint at the place."

"Can't you find a way of earning a bit? What about an extra postman's job in the Christmas holidays? Rob Beal, in my form, said that his brother did it last year and got quite decent pay."

"That would be all right if we lived in Selchester, but they don't need anybody out here. The same goes for a newspaper round. That's the worst of a one-horse hole like this."

Peter tried to think of any other kind of job Tony might be able to do. "Well, you are supposed to be jolly good at English. Why don't you have a shot at writing something for the *Gazette*? You might try an article about Samuel Cunliffe and how you saw about him in that old copy of the *Advertiser*. It ought to make a good story."

Tony looked at him in astonishment. "Well, of all the idiotic ideas that's about the worst! What do you think would happen if the *Gazette* printed it? The place would be thick with people trying to find the other gold beaker or whatever old Samuel hid. Oh, no, Pete, I want that for myself. But actually it mightn't be a bad idea to try something for the *Gazette*. I'll talk to old Smithy about it."

"Who's he?" asked Peter.

"The senior English master. He writes for the papers sometimes."

But when he asked the teacher after English the next day the result was somewhat discouraging.

"By all means write, Tony, as long as you don't let it interfere with your work. Don't forget you've got your exams coming up next summer term. It isn't likely that you will get anything published for the first few months; it takes a while to find out just what they are looking for; but it would be good experience for you, especially if you are thinking of journalism as a career."

Tony thanked him, but didn't like to explain that it was in the next few months that he wanted to earn some money. He went home feeling thoroughly disgruntled, and his irritation was increased when, after he had done his prep, he went downstairs to find Peter working on the jigsaw puzzle.

"Oh, can't we leave that until the weekend?" he protested.

"There's no need for you to do any this evening, but I shall be away at the weekend. Bill Bartlett, who is in my form, has asked me to stay with him and go to the Circus at Cratchet Hill. Dad is taking me in when he goes to the office tomorrow morning. In any case, I'm beginning to find the puzzle quite interesting, now that most of the sky is done. I have a feeling that this house is going to be a coaching inn, but I've still got to find out where these streaks of gold fit in."

"Oh, I might as well give a hand, I suppose."

For a while they worked in silence, and at the end of half an hour the whole of the roof and chimneys was done and one or two bits of wall and windows were falling into place.

"That's funny," said Peter. "I've still got a couple of pieces with tiles. Yes, they fit together. It looks like a porch or something. There's a chain hanging down the middle, so perhaps they hung a lamp on it."

"More likely to be one of those wells with a windlass for lowering the buckets and pulling them up again," said Tony. "They often had a roof over the top."

Even as he spoke something rang a bell in his brain. The ruined cottage in the woods was called 'Well Cottage'! So although they had thought that old Samuel must have drawn his water from the river, or perhaps a spring, they must have been wrong.

This didn't sound very important, but Tony remembered reading an exciting book about a tunnel leading upwards out of a well to a secret chamber of treasure!

He was going to share his idea with Peter, but he changed his mind. Peter was going into Selchester anyway, so he wouldn't be able to go to Sedgebury. It would be a wonderful triumph if he could find the stuff on his own.

He had another reason for not confiding in his young brother. Peter seemed different somehow. Ever since that weekend he'd spent with Stephen Underhill and his mother he'd seemed a bit strange. There was that queer business about the farm, for one thing. Of course he'd been an awful chump to go flying his model where it would go over the hedge, and it was a bit awkward that young Charlie Gorse had got the blame for breaking the greenhouse, but if he'd been Peter he'd have let sleeping dogs lie. Tony had supposed that Dad had paid for the repair, but a week before he happened to tell Peter about a book which one of his classmates was offering for sale, having grown tired of model-making, and Peter said he couldn't afford it, and had explained that he'd given Great Uncle George's fiver to Mr Trent to pay for the damage. But it couldn't have cost all that. It didn't make sense.

One good thing had come out of that episode. Dad and Mr Trent were no longer at each other's throats. In fact, the other evening the farmer had called at the cottage and given Dad some spring cabbage seedlings for the garden, and learning that it happened to be Mum's birthday, had returned an hour later with a big bunch of beautiful chrysanthemums for her.

Another thought occurred to him and made him glad he hadn't said anything about his latest brain-wave. Yesterday morning, when he had been grousing about the rise in moped prices, and he had said he wished he could find the buried treasure, Peter had suggested several ways in which he might be able to *earn* money. He remembered Stephen's remark on that other Saturday. 'But if you did find something it wouldn't belong to you.' It seemed that Peter now shared that view.

Now that it was October and getting colder he knew Mum would think it very queer if he asked for sand-wiches to take with him, but he set off as soon as he had helped with the breakfast china and reached Sedgebury by half past nine.

He went straight to the little shop, which was also the post office, and was pleased to find old Mrs Oke in charge.

"Good morning, Mrs Oke. May I have a bar of that chocolate, please." He paid for his purchase and put it in his pocket. "I don't expect you remember me. I came in a few weeks ago and asked you about that broken down old cottage in the woods."

"Ay, I mind you now. Seems that there's a goodish number of folks interested in Well Cottage these days. There was another young feller in here last week axing me all about it. Talked about 'is great granfer living there or summat. But I guess that would be afore my days. I did hear tell when I were a girl that it were a keeper's cottage long ago. 'Course them was the days when all the land round here – and the whole of the village, too – belonged to some Lord feller, and the woods stretched nigh on to Brinscombe, so I suppose he'd 'ave wanted keepers and such-like to take care of it and see that nobody come shooting 'is birds. But they days is gone an' the woods is free to anybody now-adays. But what makes you so keen 'bout the ol' cottage?"

"I have to write an essay at school about the old chap who lived there during the war. There was something I wanted to ask you about it, Mrs Oke. It's called 'Well Cottage', but when my brother and I had a look round the other day we didn't see a well. Is there one?"

"Good gracious, yes! The well is that deep, I mind how, when I was a girl and we had such a dry summer that the pump in the village here run dry, folks used to go running out to the cottage to draw water from there. O' course, that were afore the ol' gennelman come, and the cottage was empty."

"But where is the well?"

"Right close to the cottage, on the side nearest the river. 'Course it's all covered up with they gurt lumps of stone which come down when the bomb fell on the place. Like I told you last time, the folks in the village, they shifted everything from the garding and dug it up, thinkin' they might find all sorts of gold and such-like, but 'tweren't no good digging right up close to the walls, 'cause the old feller put a stone path there."

"I see. Thank you for telling me, Mrs Oke. I shall be able to put a well in my essay now."

He went outside, mounted his bicycle and rode slowly away from the village. Remembering Mrs Oke's reputation for liking to know all about everything that was going on, he did not take the direct path to the woods, but kept to the main road back towards his home for about half a mile, and then turned and took the grassy ride which led towards the old ford. He left his bike hidden in a thicket of holly and walked quickly through the trees until he came in sight of the ruined cottage.

As the old postmistress had said, lumps of stone had been piled up against the wall; in fact it seemed likely that the men of Sedgebury, when they dug the garden in their search for treasure, had thrown all the rocks and stone up against that end of the cottage. Worse than this, the brambles which grew in such profusion had spread their long thorny shoots all over the pile, so that it looked as impenetrable as the Sleeping Beauty's castle!

Well, having come all this way he wasn't going to give up without an effort. Pulling out his knife he opened the larger blade and started to cut a way through the brambles, severing them near the ground and tugging each shoot away. At the end of twenty minutes he had at least a dozen prickles in his fingers, but he had cleared an area about a foot square and could see the piled up rock underneath. He put his hands in a crevice and tried to tug a lump clear, but it resisted his efforts and he stopped in disgust.

What he needed was something to use as a lever. The long stick which Peter had cut to beat back the weed and clear the path to the doorway was lying on the ground and he tried that, but it just bent and broke. Tony clenched his fists in fury at his helplessness. Dad's crowbar would have been the thing for this job, but even if he borrowed it that would not be easy to bring on a bicycle.

Then he remembered the iron bar with the hook at the end which was hanging in the old chimney. That might do the trick. He hurried round and into the cottage. Yes, it was still there. Regardless of soot and rust he grabbed it and tugged, but it would not budge. He leaned over and looked upward and then he could see at once why he could not get it. It had been joined by means of an enormous nut and bolt to another bar which ran horizontally and was embedded at either end of the stonework of the chimney.

"Bother! Bother! Bother!" He swung round on his heel and stalked towards the doorway. Then he stopped dead. Coming towards him through the woods was a tall, slim boy with bright red hair; a boy he recognized as someone he had seen that term at Selchester School!

CHAPTER EIGHT

GOLD AMONG THE TREES

The two boys looked at each other in silence, but at last the newcomer spoke. "Hello! You are Rathbone, aren't you?"

"Yes, I'm Tony Rathbone. Who are you?"

"My name is Stainer – George Stainer. I only started at Selchester this term, so you wouldn't have noticed me." His voice had an Australian intonation.

"You aren't in Four A, are you? I'm sure I'd know you if you were."

"No, I'm in Five B. The English master pointed you out to me."

"Old Smithy? What on earth for?"

"Well, two of the fellows in Five B are going to be journalists, and in class last week Mr Smith told them about one of the boys in Four A who was chasing up a story about Samuel Cunliffe, the explorer. As a matter of fact, he gave you full marks for all the trouble you were taking – hunting round in old copies of the papers and that kind of thing. Afterwards I was talking to him – asking him a bit more about the story – and you went past the open door. Mr Smith said: 'That's Rathbone – the boy I was telling Haines and Bartlett about.' I've been hoping to talk to you, but I never expected to see you out here."

"I didn't expect to see anybody," said Tony with a grin. "But now I come to think of it, old Mrs Oke at the post office did say another boy had been asking questions about the cottage. She said some ancestor of yours lived here donkey's years ago."

"That's right. He was my great grandfather. It's a bit of a dump, isn't it? How are you getting on with your story, and what brings you out here again? I'd have thought that one visit would have been enough to see all that there is."

"I wanted to find the well. Mrs Oke says it's very deep and against the side of the cottage nearest to the river, but there's a mass of stone piled up there. I came inside because I remembered that old iron bar in the grate and I thought I might be able to use it to shift the stuff, but it's bolted."

George Stainer had a look and grinned. "I'll say it's bolted!" He straightened his back and stood looking round the small room. "What a place for a civilized man to live. It's worse than the shacks they build in the outback, except that this is stone, and they are mostly corrugated iron."

"The outback? You mean in Australia?"

"Yes. My grandfather went out there during the Second World War – a liaison job with the forces – and he liked the wildness of it, so afterwards he and Gran settled there with Mum. She was only a kid, of course. Dad was an Australian, too, so I guess that makes me about three quarters Aussie. Where is the well?"

"Round here." Tony led the way to the place where he had cleared away the brambles. "You see? I tried to shift that lump, and I thought I might do it if I had a lever."

"Well, let's both have a go. Only if it starts to move be ready to jump. I wouldn't want that lot on my toes or yours."

At first it seemed that even two pairs of hands would not be enough, but then it moved an inch or two.

"It's coming! Pull, Tony!"

One final effort did the trick. Both boys leapt back as

the big piece of wall, released from the position in which it had been lying for almost forty years, tumbled down the pile and came to rest on the ground three feet away. This lump, not having been crushed by anything on top of it, was by far the largest. There were still several awkward obstacles, but by the end of half an hour a section of path about ten feet long was free.

But still there was no sign of the well! "What a swizzle!" said Tony in disgust. "That old woman must have been pulling my leg." He sat down, panting. "Phew, I wish I'd brought a drink."

"Gran gave me a couple of apples," said George. "They are in one of the panniers on my bike. Let's go and get them."

They walked a little way along the path leading to the village, where George had left a shiny low-powered motorbike.

"Oo, what a beauty. Have you had it for long?"

"No. Gran bought it for me just after we got to England. We live about five miles from Selchester – at Tenworthy – and I use if for getting to school as there's no bus."

"Do you live with your grandmother?"

"Yep. You see, Grandad died about ten years ago – and Mum and Dad were killed when that cyclone hit Darwin. That was our nearest place – about three hundred miles – and Mum and Dad had gone in there on a business trip."

"How awful!" Tony tried to think what it would be like without his parents. He groused sometimes, saying that they bossed him about too much, but – ugh! It didn't bear thinking about. "What made you and your gran come to England?"

"Well, like I told you, she was British; in fact, she came from Devon; and she's getting on a bit. She could have run our place in the Northern Territory with a good manager, but I'm not really keen on farming – I want to be an engineer – so she sold out and came back." He shook himself as if to thrust sad memories away. "Well now, have you had enough, or shall we have one more go? There's still a few feet of that wall to clear. I must say I'd like to find Great Grandad's well."

"Okay." Munching their apples they returned to the cottage. "You know, it must have been there at one time. Old Mrs Oke said she remembered a summer when she was a girl, when the folk from Sedgebury had to go and draw water from it because the village well had run dry. She said the cottage was empty, so I suppose it was between the time your great grandfather lived in it and the war years when old Samuel Cunliffe was using it."

George looked at him in surprise. "But Samuel Cunliffe was my great grandad! That's why I was so much interested in your story."

"Oh!" Tony tried to work it out. "Did you know him? Old Mr Cunliffe, I mean? No, of course you didn't. He died in nineteen forty-two, just after the air raid."

"That's right. But Grandad used to tell me a lot about him. Great Grandad was a difficult chap – in fact he and Grandad used to quarrel whenever they met – and I don't think they saw each other after the old fellow went to South America."

Tony remembered that the details in the paper had only listed one son to old Samuel, and he was born in nineteen hundred. So that man must have been George's grandad, who had gone to Australia.

"What are you thinking about?" asked George with a smile.

"I was wondering what happened to everything after Mr Cunliffe died. Mrs Oke said some people came and took away all the furniture. I suppose your grandfather inherited that?"

"No. Like I said, Grandad, who was in the army, had a job in Australia during the war. I expect anything worth having was sold and Grandad got the money. I'll ask Gran sometime if you want to know for your essay. Well, let's get on with finding the disappearing well."

Tony was in a fix. George was a descendant of the explorer, so if his hunch proved correct and old Samuel had used the well as a hiding place for his treasures, anything they found would belong to George or any other members of his family. This would not suit Tony's book at all. In any case, it was pretty obvious that George didn't need money. He'd said that his grandmother had sold their farm, or whatever it was, in Australia, so she probably got a small fortune for that. He, on the other hand, wanted cash badly. He deserved it, too. He had put in a lot of work on his researches; he deserved a reward. If he hadn't started on his hunt George Stainer would not have known the first thing about the cottage.

Should he say that he'd got to get home? Then he could come back another day on his own. But suppose he did that and George remained behind and found — whatever there was to find? Perhaps he'd better stay for a bit. Rather reluctantly he went round to the wall, where George had already started again on dragging away the bits of broken stone.

Ten minutes later he unearthed a piece of iron. It was about as long as his arm and shaped like a rather flat letter 'S'.

"Oh, boy, we're getting warm!" said George. "You see what that is, Tony? It's the handle of the pump. Yep, and here's the spout that the water used to come out from. Now all we want is the upright, and if we can find out where it went into the ground we shall be home and dry!"

And soon afterwards they did find it, buckled and flattened by the weight which had fallen on it, but still with the bottom, which was set in concrete, sticking into the ground about a pace away from the wall. There was a ring of flagstones round it, similar to the ones which formed the path to the cottage door, but whether any of these would at one time have been movable it was impossible to say, as the gaps between them were packed solidly with crumbled stone and mortar.

George tried to bend the pipe upright again, but it was too strong. "Oh well, we couldn't work it anyway without the handle," he said. "But I'm glad we found it. I say, just look at the time! Gran wants me home by one o'clock. Be seeing you, Tony."

He hurried away, and Tony, after one more look round to see if there were any obvious clues to a possible hiding place, went off to find his bicycle and go back to his own meal.

It rained in the afternoon, so he watched the sport on the telly, and after supper he hunted through the bookcase to try to find the story he'd read about the treasure hidden in a well. The telephone rang and his father answered it.

"High Steadington 2478 . . . Oh, good evening, Aunt Emily. Nice to hear from you. How are you keeping?" There was a very long pause while he listened to the voice on the other end of the line and Tony grinned to himself. Aunt Emily was renowned for her non-stop chatter on the telephone. Then Dad spoke again. "Well, that will be splendid for you. Of course we don't mind. You can come to us some other time. . . . Why, yes, of course. We shall be pleased to see you. I was sorry to miss you last time. . . . Yes, they are getting on

pretty well with it, although it is quite a difficult one
... yes, I'm sure they will. Peter is away for this weekend, staying with a school friend, but Tony is here. ...
Three weeks today then. Good-bye. Love from us all."

He came back to his chair and Mum looked up from
her knitting. "What is Aunt Em's news? She sounded
quite excited."

Dad smiled. "She is. You remember hearing about
Violet Cope, who was at school with her?"

"Do I not! Aunt Em is always talking of her."

"Well, apparently Mrs Cope and her sister were
going on a Mediterranean cruise for Christmas; they'd
booked their cabin and everything; and now the sister
can't come, so Violet wants Aunt Em to go instead. She
was afraid we might be hurt, but I assured her that we
were glad for her to have the chance."

"I should think so. It will be lovely for her. Did she
say something about coming over in three weeks?"

"Yes, three weeks today. You haven't got anything
fixed, have you?" Mum shook her head. "She says she
wants to bring our Christmas presents. By the way,
Tony, you'd better get a move on with that puzzle.
She'll take it when she comes."

"Dad, we'll never get it done. It's not half way yet."

"Oh, I think you've done at least half," said Mum.
"Look, Tony, I'll give you a hand if you like, and we'll
put in an hour now. Peter can do his share on some of
the evenings next week while you are working."

His mother certainly had an eye for shapes. She put
in three pieces to Tony's one, although she was working
on the woodland down the left side, which was
much more difficult than the courtyard which he was
tackling.

"Ah, now I can see what Peter's bars of gold are!"
she said. "Don't you see, Tony? The evening sun is
shining on the trunks of some of the trees and making

them look as if they'd been touched by King Midas."
She stood back and surveyed the picture. "You know,
it's going to be lovely when it is finished. That old
bridge which the coach has just crossed, the river running through the fields in the foreground and the road
winding away into the forest."

Tony laughed at her enthusiasm, but the golden tree
trunks seemed to give him encouragement in the search
which was never far from his thoughts. Surely there
was gold hidden somewhere in or near the cottage
among the trees in Sedgebury woods!

CHAPTER NINE

DANGEROUS WATERS

Tony had been afraid that he wouldn't have another chance of going to the cottage until the following Saturday, but at lunchtime on Sunday Mum said she wanted to visit a woman who lived about five miles away and Dad offered to drive her over. As soon as they had gone he changed into his oldest jeans, armed himself with an old screwdriver and a short length of iron bar which he found in the shed and raced off on his bicycle the four miles to Sedgebury. This time he didn't go near the village, but cut straight through the woods.

In his mind he was sure that whatever Samuel Cunliffe had hidden – and there had to be something, or he wouldn't have said what he had to the reporter from the *Advertiser* – then he would find it near the well.

For half an hour he scraped away at the gaps between the flagstones, growing more and more despondent when he discovered that each one was firmly cemented to the next. Each one, that is, until he reached the one on the side nearest to the cottage – the one which formed part of the path which ran round beside the broken-down wall. Here his screwdriver went right through the gap on all four sides.

Getting more and more excited, he scraped and scrabbled until it was clear all round, then pushed his iron lever into a small space in one corner which might have been made for the purpose. It was coming! He kicked a small piece of stone under the corner he had lifted and then, exerting all his strength, he pulled up the flagstone, turned it over and laid it down carefully.

"Well, what on earth!" What he had expected to find he had no idea, but certainly not the smooth concreted surface which was exposed; a surface showing no sign that it had ever been lifted. Tony clenched his fists in fury.

But after a minute he cheered up. He was on the right track; he must be. Nobody would have made a place like that for nothing. Kneeling down, he dug the useful old screwdriver into the earth which surrounded three sides of the opening. Nothing happened. But on the fourth side, where the cement merged with the wall of the cottage, he found the solution. The moving of the stone had allowed a large lump of the cottage wall to slide downwards, leaving a space above it which was wide enough to insert his fingers. This meant that it was loose and could be pulled out. Scarcely breathing in his excitement he dragged it clear and looked into the gap. Yes, there was something at the back. He thrust in his arm, his fingers found a handle, which he tugged lustily, and he pulled out an old tin box; originally black, like the one Dad kept in the loft with papers in it, but now scratched and rusty. It was, of course, locked, but that was only to be expected. Tony lifted it carefully and shook it. It was heavy and something inside it rattled.

He had quite a job to get the flagstone back into place but at last it was done. He scattered a lot of plaster and earth into the grooves, picked up his precious find and went back to his bicycle. The journey home was difficult, because he had to balance the box on his handlebars and the box was very heavy, but he managed it without mishap. He cleaned it up as best he could with a piece of rag he found in the shed, then, as he knew Mum and Dad would be home soon, he pushed the box under his bed, changed his clothes, scrubbed his muddy fingernails and went downstairs.

At bedtime he pulled it out again and tried to open it with a few odd keys he had, but it was obvious that this was not going to be possible. He would have to break it open, and even that would be difficult. In the meantime he must put it somewhere where Mum wouldn't find it, and also where Peter would not see it. Now that it was actually in his possession he felt increasingly certain that his young brother would say that George Stainer had more right to it.

In the end he solved that problem by taking down his suitcase, which was kept on top of the wardrobe, and putting the box inside that.

The next few days were terribly frustrating. He thought of taking the box out to the shed and banging a hole in it with a hammer, but knew that the noise he made would give rise to a lot of awkward questions. He might be able to drill some holes in it, but as all the good tools belonged either to Dad or to Peter he was afraid he might break something and give away his secret that way.

It was on Thursday that he had a brainwave. The school went in for a lot of handicrafts, including not only carpentry but also metal work. After lunch he went along to the building where this was done, which at that time of day was empty. He looked round quickly. Tools of all sizes and descriptions hung on the walls, and almost at once he saw just what he needed; a strong metal bar about as long as a pencil, tapered at one end to an edge about as thick as a postcard. He took it down and put it in his pocket.

That evening, leaving Peter busy with the jigsaw, he went up to do his prep, then took out the box, thrust the metal bar in under the lid in the front and levered it until at last the lock gave. With trembling fingers he opened it and peered inside.

It was full of papers – thick batches of foolscap, covered with scrawled handwriting, crossed out and corrected until in some places it looked almost illegible. Tony dragged it out impatiently. Something in the box had rattled and it certainly wasn't paper.

He was just lifting the last of it – a large envelope – when he was interrupted.

"Tony, haven't you finished yet? Supper's ready. I say, what ever is that?"

Tony looked at him with a frown. "Don't make such a row. Shut the door." Peter obeyed and came to look down at the box. "This is old Samuel Cunliffe's hidden treasure. I found it last Sunday. But I've only just got it open, and as far as I can see it's only papers. No, here's something else." He picked up some bits of dull greyish metal. "It feels like lead."

Peter, more interested in metals, snatched one up, took a pair of nail scissors off the dressing-table and scratched it. "Lead, my foot! It's what you wanted. It's gold! Where did you find the box?"

"I'll tell you about it when we come to bed. Don't breathe a word to Mum and Dad. We'd better get down to supper."

Mrs Rathbone was agreeably surprised that evening when her younger son went to bed at the first time of asking, but when Tony, too, pleaded weariness and followed him she looked anxious.

"I hope they are feeling all right," she said to her husband.

Mr Rathbone laughed. "Of course they are all right. If you ask me, I think it was just that they are bored with that puzzle. Now don't you go and do it all for them, Doris. I said they were to make it because of their rudeness to Aunt Em when she came in August." He got up and looked at it. "My word, it's an enormous thing, isn't it? It's clever though. I wonder who painted the original picture. I like the colouring of different parts of the river; bright and sparkling when the sun catches it and murky and dangerous where it is shaded by the trees. It would be easy enough to drown there, I should think."

Mrs Rathbone laughed, put in one more piece and tore herself away. "It's very fascinating, but an awful time waster. Help me to put it back, Arthur, will you, please. I think the boys left it out in the hope that they would come down tomorrow to find it nearly finished!"

Meanwhile, up in the bedroom, the boys were examining Tony's find, while he gave Peter a description of the hiding-place. He left out any mention of George. After all, he told himself, George had helped to clear the path and find the well, but the discovery of the secret cavity in the thickness of the wall was all his own doing.

Altogether there were seven of the little pieces of gold. Tony weighed the metal in his hand. "I wonder how much it is worth, and how will be the best way to sell it."

"I don't see how you can sell it at all unless you say where you found it," replied Peter. "Any jeweller is bound to want to know where you got hold of it."

"I know." Tony started to undress and then, as he got into his pyjamas, he thought of an idea. "Perhaps I could say that an old relative – an uncle or somebody like that – had worked in the goldfields of South Africa and had just died and left me these in his will. I'll think of something anyway. Come on, Pete, we'd better shove it away and get to bed."

He returned the gold to the box and Peter picked up the thick bundle of paper. "What are you going to do with this?"

"Chuck it away, I suppose. I haven't looked at it yet.

Bung it in for now and I'll have a squint at it tomorrow."

He pushed the box back under his bed and five minutes later they were both in. He lay for about half an hour making plans. He was agreeably surprised that Peter had raised no objection to the idea that as he had found the box the contents belonged to him. He hadn't been too sure of his brother's attitude.

"Tony!"

"Peter, I thought you were asleep."

"No, I've been thinking. Tony, you can't do it."

"Can't do what?"

"You can't keep that gold. It's stealing."

"Oh, rot! Finders Keepers."

"Yes, but if you hang on to the gold you can't do anything with the papers, and as old Mr Cunliffe thought them important enough to put them away in his hidey-hole they are probably something about his explorations. After all, he was a famous man. It might be something that ought to be published."

"Well, the world has done without it for nearly forty years, so I guess it won't miss it now. I'm keeping the gold and I shall shove the papers in the incinerator in the garden tomorrow, so that's that. Shut up and go to sleep!"

He turned his back on the other bed, punched up his pillow and pulled the bedding up to his chin. That would settle Peter. For a while he lay there, knowing by the restless movement that his young brother was still awake, but at last he drifted off to an uneasy sleep.

It seemed no time then before Mum opened the door and switched on the light. "Half past seven, boys. Hurry up!"

Tony groaned, but then, remembering the excitement that the day might bring, hurried into the bathroom. When he got back Peter was dressed and kneeling beside his bed; a habit which he had started since the episode at the Trent's farm. Usually Tony regarded him with tolerant amusement – after all, it was harmless enough if he wanted to be so childish – but this morning he felt slightly uneasy. There was something in his brother's attitude which suggested that his prayer was important; as if he was asking for help.

He was brushing his hair when Peter got up. "Tony, while you were in the bathroom I had another look at those papers. Do you know what they are?" Tony shook his head. "Well, I'm not sure, of course, but I think it is a copy – probably the one he wrote first, before he did one to send to be typed – of the book which was destroyed by bombs. There is a big envelope full of photographs and they are numbered, to say where they ought to come. You know what the librarian said about him. His book would be tremendously important."

Tony was furious. He didn't want to hear about the papers.

"I told you last night to shut up. Who do you think you are – telling me what to do or not to do? Just because you think you are good."

"I don't think I'm good. But I do know now that Jesus Christ helps people if they ask Him. That's what I did when I was in such a mess about breaking that greenhouse and Charlie Gorse getting the blame. Look, why don't you – why don't you be decent about this? Tell Dad all about it – how you found it and what you've got. He would be able to say what you ought to do."

"And you know what he'd say, don't you? Dad's a lawyer and he'd insist on finding out what old Samuel put in his will and so on. It would take months and I probably wouldn't get a penny for all the work I've done."

Peter bit his lip. "Well, I'm sorry, Tony," he said slowly, "but if you won't promise to tell Dad, then I shall. Not at breakfast, of course; there wouldn't be time – but this evening."

Tony's clenched fist landed on the side of Peter's head with a thump and the boy was sent sprawling. "You rotten little sneak." Then he stopped, appalled at himself. Peter was three years his junior and half a head shorter. "I'm sorry. I shouldn't have hit you. You can get up; I won't touch you again." He turned on his heel and stalked out of the room and down to breakfast.

"Peter dear, you are looking very pale this morning. Why, your ear is all swollen. Have you got earache?"

"No, I'm all right, Mum. I – fell over in the bedroom."

"Would you rather stay at home today?"

"No, thanks, Mum. We've got the form gym competitions today."

"Don't fuss about the boy, Doris." Dad, never at his brightest in the mornings, looked up from his paper. "Which is your favourite bit of apparatus, Peter? Mine used to be the horse."

"Mine is the rings, Dad. Sergeant Judson, who takes us, said I might get into the team if I do well today. We take on Taunton School in three weeks' time."

Nothing more was said. Before running for the bus Tony went up to the bedroom, replaced the tin box in his suitcase and fetched the metal tool he had borrowed. He must make a chance to return it during lunch.

The brothers walked in silence to the bus, and as soon as the next boys got on, a mile nearer to Selchester, Peter joined one of them, who was in his form, and they started to discuss the gym competition.

It was half way through the afternoon, during the

maths lesson, that the headmaster's secretary entered the Four A classroom and went to speak to the master. He listened and nodded, and the woman left.

"Rathbone, you are wanted in the headmaster's study. You can go right away."

Tony's heart thumped uncomfortably as he walked along the corridors, into the front hall and tapped on Mr Bailey's door. Could the head have heard about the gold? It didn't seem possible, but Tony couldn't think of any other reason for the summons.

"Come in! Ah, Rathbone! I sent for you to tell you that your young brother has met with an accident. We don't know how serious it is yet, but he is unconscious and we have sent for an ambulance to take him to hospital."

Tony's mouth felt dry. "What happened, sir?"

"He was doing his routine on the rings, and Sergeant Judson says he seemed suddenly to lose his grip and he fell."

"He knocked himself out, sir? Did he land on his head?"

"No, that is the odd thing about it. The sergeant says that he was able partly to break the boy's fall, and in fact he came down on his side, but it almost looked as if he was giddy and lost consciousness while he was still upside down on the rings. I sent for you because I thought it would be better if you telephoned your father. He works in Selchester, I believe."

Tony nodded and was dismissed. He telephoned his father from the secretary's office next door and went back to the class. He sat staring at the blackboard, but he did not see the complicated geometrical problem. The picture in front of his eyes was of Peter falling to the bedroom floor after a cowardly blow on the side of his head.

CHAPTER TEN

THROUGH THE DARK FOREST

That weekend was the most miserable Tony had ever known. A dozen times a day he almost confessed to Mum or Dad that Peter had fallen in the bedroom because he had knocked him down. He kept remembering a time when he had caught his ear a sharp knock on a goal post in a scrimmage during a game of football, and felt giddy on and off for a day or two afterwards. The doctor had explained that there was a close connection between your sense of balance and the delicate mechanism of the ear. And his clenched fist had caught Peter full force on one of his.

But although he felt he would like to confess and get it off his chest – even if it meant a ghastly row – two things stopped him. First, if he admitted that he had knocked Peter down, his parents would want to know what had caused the argument, and second, his mum and dad took it for granted that it was just a fall; that perhaps the boy had tripped and knocked his head on a corner of the dressing-table; and they were so worried that it seemed unkind to add to their trouble.

At assembly on Monday morning – the one day of the week when the whole school came together in the big hall – the head mentioned Peter Rathbone in the prayers, asking God for the boy's complete recovery, and afterwards Tony was surrounded by his formmates, who had not heard of the accident.

"No, I haven't heard anything this morning. Yesterday he was still unconscious. My father was going to

THROUGH THE DARK FOREST 77

the hospital on his way to work and I'm going to phone his office during lunch."

The first lesson that morning was his favourite, English, and the second was a free period in which, in theory, the boys were supposed to work on any subject at which they were slow. As Mr Smith was leaving the Four A classroom he beckoned to Tony.

"How is the essay on Samuel Cunliffe coming on, Tony?" he asked. "I am looking forward to reading it." They were in the corridor by this time and boys and girls were scurrying past on their way to the science laboratories or the gymnasium.

"I haven't written anything yet, sir." Tony felt that he never wanted to think about the explorer again.

"Still researching, eh? I can understand that you cannot concentrate on anything like that at present. You and your parents must be very worried about your young brother. They and you will be in my prayers during this anxious time."

Tony looked at him with a frown. "Do you think it does any good, sir? Prayers like the Head's this morning, I mean? Do you think it would make the least difference if everybody in the school prayed for Peter?"

"Of course I do, Tony. Don't you remember the story of your brother's famous namesake, the Apostle Peter? He was thrown into prison by Herod, who intended to have him executed after Easter. The Bible says: 'Earnest prayer for him was made to God by the church.' And you know what happened, don't you? God sent his angel to bring Peter out of prison miraculously. Of course God doesn't always act that way, but it is an example of what prayer can do. You go on praying for your brother, Tony, and you can be sure that God will act in the way that is best."

"Oh, I can't pray, sir. God wouldn't listen to me. It was my fault that it happened at all."

Pupils were still surging past and quiet conversation was impossible. Mr Smith opened the door of the next classroom and pushed Tony in. "Four B are in the chemistry lab for this period," he said as he closed the door. "Why was it your fault?"

"I punched him on the ear and knocked him down. He told Mum and Dad that he'd fallen – which was true as far as it went – Peter isn't the sort to sneak – at least not about a thing like that."

"Would you like to tell me about it? This is one of my free periods, too." Mr Smith did not mention that he had intended to spend it in the masters' common room correcting Five A's essays! "What you say will go no further."

It was difficult to begin, but then the whole story came pouring out. "So you see, sir, it wasn't really that I was keen to dig into old Samuel Cunliffe's past for the sake of – of writing about it. It was just that I thought from that bit in the old *Advertiser* that he'd probably got some Inca gold hidden away somewhere and I wanted to get my hands on it."

"Are you so very short of money?"

"Oh, I get quite decent pocket money, sir. Dad isn't mean." He told the master about the moped he wanted and then added: "I know it says somewhere in the Bible that money is the root of all evil, and how right it is."

"Will you boys never learn not to misquote!"

Tony looked at him with a faint grin, knowing well that misquotation was, according to the English master, one of the worst crimes a boy could commit. But he was puzzled.

"Isn't that what it says, sir? I thought it did."

"No, it is not. What the Bible says is not just 'money', but 'love of money'. It is when the desire for money becomes the most important thing in life – in other words, when money becomes your idol – then it is evil. But tell me, Tony. You said your brother went with you on that first search at the cottage, but now he seems not to want any further part in it, and is even prepared to tell your father rather than allow you to benefit from it. What changed his attitude?"

"I don't quite know, sir, but Peter got in a hole, too, and since then he's been different." He told Mr Smith what he knew of the episode at the farm. "When I accused him last Friday of being goody-goody he said he wasn't good, but he asked Jesus Christ every day to help him, and he hoped he was better than he used to be." He frowned thoughtfully. "I think Christ must have listened to him, too, sir, and helped him on Friday. It must have taken a lot of guts to say he'd tell Dad. Like I said, Peter isn't a sneak."

"I agree. Well, Jesus Christ answered Peter's prayer. Why do you think He would not answer yours if you asked Him?"

"Well, it's different, isn't it, sir? I behaved so badly; much worse than Peter."

"It isn't the degree of wrong-doing which matters so much, Tony, but the genuine desire to be forgiven. The Bible says in several places that Jesus Christ came to seek and to save. He said it wasn't the strong, healthy people who needed to be healed but the sick ones. But of course if you are ill and you won't call in the doctor he can't do anything to make you better, can he? If we will call in Jesus Christ; will admit that we can't help ourselves; then He will save us. There is a lovely verse in Paul's letter to the Ephesians which reads: 'For by grace you have been saved, through faith; and this is not your own doing; it is the gift of God.' We can't make ourselves good, but if we will turn to Christ and tell Him we are sorry for what we have done wrong, then by His grace – and if you look that up in the dictionary you will find that it means unmerited favour – by His grace He will save us."

The rushing from one class to another had ended, and here in Four B it was very quiet as Tony tried to understand fully just what Mr Smith had said, and then to decide whether, as the English master put it, to call in the Doctor! He was a proud boy. He knew he had brains and he intended to do well in life. It would be hard to tell Mum and Dad what he had done, and also to lose his last chance to get enough cash for his share of the moped. He wanted that motorbike so badly.

Mr Smith glanced at his watch. "I must get along. Essay correction, like time and tide, waits for no man! As I said, your mum and dad, your brother and you, Tony, will be in my prayers in these difficult days."

"Thank you, sir." There seemed to be nothing else to say. He had told old Smithy that it was no good praying for him, but it was a nice feeling that the prayers would still be offered.

Restlessly he walked over to the window and stood looking down at the roof of the gymnasium building in the courtyard below, and he seemed to see Peter, lying unconscious on the floor.

"Oh, Lord!" He leaned his head against the cool glass of the window and closed his eyes. "O Lord, please answer everyone's prayers for Peter. And please help me, too. I'm in such a muddle."

Presently the clanging of a bell recalled him to himself. The period was over and Four B would be returning to their room. He went back to Four A next door and sat through forty minutes of French, but it could not be said that he took in a single word. The French master, aware, as all the people in the school were, of the accident to Peter, took one look at his blank expression and left him alone.

Then it was time for school dinner. Tony could push and grab with the best of them, but that day he didn't care if he ate or not, so he went and telephoned to his father instead. Dad said that Peter's condition was unchanged.

The first sitting of lunch was just finishing, so Tony lined up for the second one. He wasn't hungry, but he supposed he'd better eat. As he was leaving the room afterwards he found himself beside George Stainer.

"Hello, Tony! What's the latest news of your brother? You and your folk must be going through a very worrying time." Tony repeated the information he had received from his father, and George, after one look at the unhappy face beside his, decided to change the subject. "Have you been out to the cottage since we met there?"

Looking back afterwards, it seemed to Tony that this must have been Jesus Christ's answer to his prayer for help. He had either got to lie again or tell George the whole truth, and he had had a sickener of lies.

"I want to tell you about that. Where can we go to get away from the mob?"

"The bike shed, I should think. There won't be anybody there."

The sight of George's shiny motor-bike made Tony grit his teeth. He turned resolutely and sat down on an old wooden bench. "Yes, I went out there on the day after we found the well. George, you know your great grandfather wrote a book which was never published because of the air-raids?"

"No, I don't think Grandad ever mentioned that. Tell me about it."

So Tony told him all that he had learned about the old man and then, with a deep breath, he added: "Well, I guessed from that article that the old chap had hidden something away, and as it obviously wasn't anywhere inside the cottage, and old Mrs Oke said that the village chaps dug up all the garden, I somehow guessed that it might be near the well. That was the real reason why I wanted to find out where the well had been."

He stopped again and George demanded impatiently: "Was it?"

"Yes. I found it." He described the details of the hiding-place. "It was an old tin box, and inside were a lot of papers and some little bits of gold. It was Peter who looked at the papers and he said he thought it was the original manuscript of the book."

"Yippee! How super! You are a real pal, Tony. Although Grandad used to quarrel with his father he was very proud of him; I wish he could have known about this."

Once again the temptation to pretend that there was nothing wrong in what he had done was very strong.

But then George added: "It might have been lost for ever if you hadn't gone seeking for it."

To seek and to save! That was what old Smithy had said about Jesus Christ. "Yes, but you haven't heard it all yet. I didn't mean to give it to you. I intended to burn the papers, chuck away the box, sell the gold and keep the cash. Now you know what kind of a pal I am."

Once he had started it was easier to go on. George listened in silence, but when the story was finished he smiled.

"I'm glad you told me. I had an idea, that morning at Sedgebury, that there was some hurdle which was keeping us from being pals. What made you change your mind about telling me?"

"Something old Smithy said. As a matter of fact Pete talked about it, too." In halting sentences he tried to explain about the help his brother had said Jesus Christ had given him, and how he himself had asked for help. "I suppose that sounds idiotic to you?"

"Of course it doesn't. I put my trust in the Lord Jesus when I was twelve. I don't know how Gran and I would have got on when Mum and Dad were killed if we hadn't been Christians. Oh, I'm longing to see that manuscript."

Nothing more was said then, but Tony felt as if he had been journeying through the darkest part of the jigsaw's forest and was now almost reaching the trees which were bright with evening sunshine.

Not that he was there yet. There was still the confession to his parents, which followed that evening. It was an awful half hour, but at last they understood and he felt that he was forgiven.

Mum suggested that perhaps George might like to spend the next evening with them; he could have Peter's bed and Peter's seat on the bus. Tony had just finished a call to George's grandmother, to get permission for this, when the phone rang again. It was the hospital, ringing to say that Peter had regained consciousness. Although he was dazed and suffering severe headache, they were well pleased with his condition and hoped that he would be able to return home in a few days' time.

CHAPTER ELEVEN

JOURNEYING ON

Aunt Emily arrived for lunch as arranged on the first Saturday in December. She was tremendously excited about her coming voyage and the boys found her much more interesting than usual. Instead of a recital of her aches and pains she was full of details about the places she hoped to visit.

But all the same, by the time the meal was finished both Tony and Peter felt that they had had enough.

"We'll wash up, Mum," said Tony.

"Oh, thank you, boys; that would be a help." There was a note in Mum's voice which told them she was not fooled by this unusual offer and they smiled when they got into the kitchen.

But as he thrust a pile of spoons and forks into the hot water Tony looked at his brother with a puzzled frown. "Pete, am I imagining things, or have you noticed that Mum and Dad have changed lately? Dad doesn't bite our heads off every time he's feeling fed up about something, and Mum seems to see the funny side of everything – like she did just then."

"Um-yes. But perhaps it's because we are different. For instance, yesterday when Mum wanted Dad to get some logs in, you offered to go and fetch them instead."

"Oh well, I knew he was watching that law case on telly, and it didn't interest me much," said Tony defensively. "And what about you? Who took those papers up to the farm this morning instead of scooting off to the shed to get on with model-making?"

Peter grinned rather sheepishly. "Oh well! Anyway, Mrs Trent was baking and she gave me a super hot yeast bun." Then he looked more serious. "Do you think it will always be like this now? I mean, no more rows and no more problems?"

Tony shook his head decisively. "No, I don't. Just because people are Christians that doesn't mean that they'll never have troubles. Look at George. He lost his mum and dad in that awful Darwin cyclone, and that was after he became a Christian."

"Yes. And I remember now, when Stephen's mum was talking about it. She said she had an awful temper and I wanted to know if she stopped losing it when she asked Jesus Christ to look after her, and she said she didn't – not all at once – but He made her feel so ashamed of herself that she wanted to put things right afterwards."

Tony nodded. "I think that's it. If you belong to Christ you've got to keep on asking Him to help you." His train of thought was interrupted by the sight of a motorbike being ridden past the kitchen window and coming to a halt outside the garage doors. "Hello, here's George."

He flung open the back door and his friend came in, pulling off his thick gloves and his crash helmet. He grinned at them.

"Well well, you are busy! Let me wash my hands and I'll take over from Peter, while he shoves the things away."

The two Rathbones demanded to know the reason for his visit, but he just smiled teasingly and refused to tell them until the washing up was done. "Your dad will want to hear it, too, so there's no point in saying it twice over," he said provokingly.

Back in the living-room he was introduced to Aunt Emily and listened politely while she told him of her forthcoming holiday, and then he turned to Mr Rathbone and produced a thick envelope.

"You were so good about helping Gran and me to find out about my great grandfather's lawyers, sir, that I thought you'd like to see this right away," he said.

Tony and Peter waited eagerly while their father read the letter. "That's splendid!" Dad looked at the others. "Mr Fothergill, who is the senior partner of the firm of solicitors who dealt with old Samuel Cunliffe's Will, says that there is absolutely no doubt of the authenticity of the manuscript which Tony found in the old deed box. He has shown it to one of the foremost British publishers, and they have agreed, in these unusual circumstances, to arrange to have it typed and put in order, and will publish it as soon as they can do so, probably in the Spring. They say that the information contained is of very great value, throwing new light on many aspects of the old Inca civilization, and in their opinion the book will become a standard work of reference all over the world."

The result of this revelation was, of course, that Aunt Emily had to be told the whole story, and Tony and Peter, who had always regarded their old great aunt as rather helpless and a bit dim, were surprised at her interest.

"You must let me know when it comes out, Arthur, and I will certainly buy a copy. Did you say that you are Mr Cunliffe's only descendant, George? The book should provide you with a good income for some years to come, I should think."

"Yes, Miss Rathbone, the letter says that there ought to be quite a lot of money coming in from royalties when it is published. Of course it will come to my grandmother first, because Grandfather left everything to her." He looked at Tony. "Gran says that you are to have ten per cent of the profits because you found the manuscript."

Tony went scarlet. For a moment the offer was very tempting. Then the memories of all that had happened came flooding back into his mind. "It's very good of her, George, but I'd rather not. It's been exciting, but I can't take payment. You know I can't."

There was a pause and then George nodded. "I understand. But won't you take enough to pay your share towards your moped?"

Somehow the refusal came more easily that time. "No, thank you, George. As a matter of fact, old Smithy has got me a job for ten days in the Christmas holidays, provided I can get in to Selchester. I hadn't said anything about it yet, because I wanted to ask Dad if I can come in and out with him. It's at the offices of the *Gazette* – they want an extra hand for a lot of cataloguing – and they will pay me two pounds a day, so I shall easily be able to raise the cash. That will be all right, won't it, Dad?"

"How many hours will you be working?"

"Only four hours a day – from nine until one – on the book work, but they have said that if I like I can go round with Mr Hepburn, one of their reporters, in the afternoons, as an unpaid assistant, which will give me enough experience to know whether I want a career in journalism or not."

Naturally Aunt Emily then wanted to know about the moped, and although she shook her head at the idea, saying that motor cycles were noisy, smelly, dangerous things, she certainly approved of Tony's plan to earn his share.

"You will appreciate it much more if you have worked for it," she said, again surprising the boys by her unexpected wisdom.

Mum reminded them that they hadn't shown the old

lady the jigsaw, so Tony and George went into the cupboard and carried out the long table top.

"My goodness, what a big one it is! I didn't realize that I was setting you boys such a task." She put on her other spectacles and looked at it carefully. "What a lovely picture. The end of one part of a journey and the horses being brought out ready for the next stage! You know, although I suppose cars are easier and quicker, there must have been something very romantic about coach travel."

Tony's eyes met Peter's. 'The end of one part of a journey and the beginning of the next.' It was the same for both of them. Until recently they had gone their own way, living their own, sometimes lawless lives. Now they were beginning a new stage. But this time Someone else was in charge. And although no doubt the road would be difficult in places, they could trust Him to bring them safely to their destination.